MYSTERY AT
LANE'S END

Other Doubleday Signal Books

BONNIE
PONY OF THE SIOUX
THE JUNGLE SECRET
NORTH POLE: THE STORY OF ROBERT
  PEARY
BASEBALL BONUS KID
CAROL HEISS: OLYMPIC QUEEN
GREEN LIGHT FOR SANDY
SEA TREASURE
THE BLOOD RED BELT
KENDALL OF THE COAST GUARD
RODEO ROUNDUP
NANCY KIMBALL, NURSE'S AIDE
FOOTBALL FURY
CIVIL WAR SAILOR
DINNY AND DREAMDUST
AUSTIN OF THE AIR FORCE
THE LONG REACH
FOOTLIGHTS FOR JEAN
BASEBALL SPARK PLUG
RUNAWAY TEEN
LIGHTNING ON ICE
HOT ROD THUNDER
JUDY NORTH, DRUM MAJORETTE
DIRT TRACK DANGER
ADVENTURE IN ALASKA
CLIMB TO THE TOP
FISHING FLEET BOY
JACK WADE, FIGHTER FOR LIBERTY
THE MYSTERY OF HIDDEN HARBOR
SCANLON OF THE SUB SERVICE
A SUMMER TO REMEMBER
NAT DUNLAP, JUNIOR "MEDIC"
BLAST-OFF! A TEEN ROCKET
  ADVENTURE
TWO GIRLS IN NEW YORK
THE MYSTERY OF THE FLOODED
  MINE
CATHY AND LISETTE
EVANS OF THE ARMY
HIGH SCHOOL DROP OUT

DOUBLE TROUBLE
PRO FOOTBALL ROOKIE
THE MYSTERY OF BLUE STAR LODGE
ADVENTURE IN DEEPMORE CAVE
FAST BALL PITCHER
HI PACKETT, JUMPING CENTER
NURSE IN TRAINING
SHY GIRL: THE STORY OF ELEANOR
  ROOSEVELT
SKI PATROL
BIG BAND
GINNY HARRIS ON STAGE
GRACIE
THREE CHEERS FOR POLLY
SECOND YEAR NURSE
FEAR RIDES HIGH
THE MYSTERY OF THE INSIDE ROOM
ARTHUR ASHE: TENNIS CHAMPION
THE MYSTERY OF THE THIRD-HAND
  SHOP
GOING, GOING, GONE
THE KID FROM CUBA: ZOILO
  VERSALLES
GANG GIRL
TV DANCER
ROAR OF ENGINES
DONNA deVARONA: GOLD MEDAL
  SWIMMER
PETE CASS: SCRAMBLER
BLACK SOLDIER
TROUBLE AT MERCY HOSPITAL
TRAPPED IN SPACE
MARTIN LUTHER KING: FIGHTER FOR
  FREEDOM
DANCE! THE STORY OF KATHERINE
  DUNHAM
QUEEN OF ENGLAND: THE STORY OF
  ELIZABETH I
THE TOMMY DAVIS STORY
FIRST LADY OF INDIA: THE STORY
  OF INDIRA GANDHI

MYSTERY
AT LANE'S END

EVELYN FIORE

Illustrated By
Harold James

A DOUBLEDAY SIGNAL BOOK
Doubleday & Company, Inc.
Garden City, New York

LIBRARY OF CONGRESS CATALOG CARD NUMBER 69–11003
COPYRIGHT © 1968 BY DOUBLEDAY & COMPANY, INC.
ALL RIGHTS RESERVED
PRINTED IN THE UNITED STATES OF AMERICA
PREPARED BY **B** RUTLEDGE BOOKS
FIRST EDITION

CONTENTS

CHAPTER 1

THE FIRST NIGHT

Patty Mason stepped off the train at Pinewood station, full of hope, a little bit frightened. What would her new job be like?

"They told us it would be quite an adventure," she said to her two new friends, Ken Smith and Myra Collins, who were following close behind her. "Now we find out."

A tall, attractive girl, Patty was just eighteen. Her dark blond hair, cut short, was lightened on top by the sun, and her tanned skin made her eyes look deeper blue. She was in high spirits, even though the summer evening was dark and rainy, and the town didn't look very inviting.

Patty and her two new friends were Vistas. "Vista" was the short name for "Volunteer Workers in Service to America." Patty had joined this organization because "We have to do something right here in the United

States," as she had explained to her parents. "If things don't get better fast, they are going to get worse a lot faster."

Patty had seen with her own eyes that people with a low income, or no income at all, were getting restless and angry. There were not enough jobs for them that paid enough to live on, not enough training programs to help people get better jobs, not enough good schools for the children. Whole neighborhoods had gone to pieces. Kids dropped out of school, where they had learned hardly anything anyway because classes were too crowded. They hung around street corners, bored and almost sure to get into trouble.

Patty got along well with kids, and she was hoping that Vista would give her a chance to work with children. After a training course that lasted six weeks, she was ready to go to work. In Vista's New York offices she had met Myra and Ken. Now they were in Pinewood.

A young man came up to the little group and introduced himself. "I'm John Simmons from Lane's End House." He shook hands, first with Patty, then with Myra and Ken.

John was tall and bony, with wild hair and a pleasant face, and Patty liked him on sight. "Boy, am I glad to see you!" he said. "I sure hope one of you can

drive that station wagon—it has a floor shift. Because
if you can't, we have rather a long walk ahead of us."

Back home in Wisconsin, Patty had often driven her
father's pick-up truck, so she could handle a floor shift
car. "I can drive, if you like," she offered. "But what's
the matter—didn't you drive to the station?"

John nodded. "But I wasn't sure I would get here." He held out a pair of broken eye glasses. "I was coaching some kids in a basketball game and got hit on the nose. There went my glasses. I barely made it to the station without them, and it was still light then. I didn't have time to pick up my spare pair from the settlement.

"They play rough around here, do they?" Ken said as they all piled into the car.

John gave him a long look. "You can say that again."

Patty felt a little uneasy. She started the car and began to inch through the down town traffic, then along strange streets that were wet and slippery. John gave her directions. He seemed unsure of himself, probably because he couldn't see properly, and that made Patty nervous.

"How far is it to Lane's End?" she asked him.

"Oh, another couple of miles. It's in the Spanish neighborhood, toward the edge of town. And you might as well get used to the new name the place has. The neighborhood people have taken to calling it Dead End, and the name has stuck."

"Dead End?" Myra and Ken said it at the same time. "What a strange name." Myra went on. "Makes you think of some place in the middle of nowhere."

"Makes *me* think of a jail. Or the death house— that's what it sounds like," Ken broke in.

"Oh, cut it out," Myra said with impatience. "You and your sick ideas."

Patty had to agree with her friend. She had wondered about Ken in the brief time she had known him. He was a good looking boy, born and raised in New York City. Judging from his talk, his parents had plenty of money and he was going on to college. But he seemed to look on social work in a run-down neighborhood as a form of fun. Something that would "look good in my record," as he kept saying. "No doubt about it," Patty thought, "Ken is out for himself, first and last."

With Myra, Patty had felt immediately at home. Myra was a small, quick, sensible girl from Maine, whose enormous glasses sat on a pretty nose that she never seemed to powder. Myra did not care for Ken either. "I think he looks down on just about everybody," she had told Patty.

"Look," John said, "our place happens to be at the end of the street—in other words, a dead end. Also, the people in the area think that our efforts to help them have more or less failed. To them, that's another dead end."

There was a moment's silence. Then John said, "I hope Grace is back by the time we get there. You know —Grace Pascoe, in charge of Lane's End."

Patty had heard a great deal about Grace Pascoe. She

was a woman famous in her field and had done social work all over the world. Now she was testing her ideas at Lane's End. "How she must hate that new name, Dead End House," Patty thought.

They were driving now through dark, wet streets on this hot, sticky July evening. Patty saw out of the corner of her eye that Ken was looking out the window. "Man, this is awful!" he said. "What do you do for kicks around here?"

Patty kept staring straight ahead, but she could almost feel the look that John gave him. She was pretty sure John wouldn't like Ken's kind of talk. In fact, she decided, it might be hard to like Ken, himself.

"We are coming into our part of town now," John said, ignoring Ken. He pointed to the rows of sad little frame houses under the yellow street lights, where sagging porches, broken window panes, and garbage cans that were too full all showed that "our part of town" was pretty grim.

From some dark houses came the blue gleam of turned on TV sets. Patty wondered—not for the first time—what people who had so little to spend for food and shelter had to give up to buy a TV set. TV must be more important than anything else in their lives.

"Some of the lucky families—the ones with half way steady incomes—got flats in a new apartment project we will be driving through," John went on. "Lots of your people will be from there. But you'll find plenty of homes with no father, or a sick mother, or very little English spoken. Most of the people speak Spanish. Many are on relief. Put in a few days trying to help and, believe me, you won't feel much like going out and swinging."

The three young people nodded. Two months ago Patty would have thought a "home with no father" meant that the father had died. Now she knew it could mean a home the father had walked out of. Or a home where there never had been a father—only a mother who had babies without bothering, or perhaps without being asked, to marry the man who was their father. A sick woman might mean she had some disease, or was crippled—but it might also mean a woman who was mentally ill, or who drank or took drugs, and neglected her children.

"Watch it!" Ken said sharply. "You almost hit that cat!"

Patty eased her grip on the wheel. "Do you want to drive? It's got to be either you or me."

"Here's that project," John broke in. "It's a pity all these buildings look like so many cereal boxes, but it is much better than what most of these families had before."

Ken stuck his head out the window. "There's not much wrong with the buildings, but why do people always drape their wash on the balconies? Why make it look like a slum when it doesn't have to?"

"Because they can't afford clothes driers, that's why!" Myra said. "And the driers that the builder puts in the basement are either jammed up or not working. And there's always wash because there are a dozen kids in each family . . ."

John spoke up. "What really bothers me about our set-up is why the neighborhood people won't come to Lane's End when we are offering everything we can think of that would give them a break."

"Won't come?" Patty was shocked.

John leaned forward to see where they were. "Quick left, then first right," he said. "No. Won't come. I suppose I ought to brief you before you meet Grace Pascoe. So you'll know what she's really like—not what she's like right now."

From what John said, Lane's End was a small settlement house in a poor part of Pinewood. About a year before, the church and several welfare agencies had decided to turn it into a really useful, lively community center for the benefit of the many new families that were crowding into the neighborhood.

"Grace is well known, and when she came here as

director everybody thought the settlement would turn into something great." John sighed. "She got things off to a fine start. The lectures and classes and things she set up—languages, cooking, the works. Then somehow, right after I started . . ."

He made a thumbs-down gesture. "The people quit coming. Like we had a disease or something. Now it's only the kids that come—sometimes. Things go wrong. . . . Hey, Patty, we turn right here."

Patty signaled and made the turn. John was saying: "Grace has all the experience in the world, but sometimes I think it's not the right kind. She's used to—well, things you see in movies, like being the only white family in a village of natives."

"Bringing the light of civilization into the dark corners of the earth," Ken said.

John nodded. "Strangely enough, you've hit the nail on the head. But these people aren't 'natives,' grateful for a little attention from their ruler. They are human beings in trouble, and trying to get out of it. Sometimes I think Grace doesn't have the right touch. Anyway, now she's a nervous wreck—and scared, too, I think."

"Scared?" Myra leaned forward in her seat. "What's there to be scared about?"

"Fires," John said. "Quite a few small ones, and sure as anything the do-it-yourself kind. Broken windows, and kids falling downstairs and their parents threatening to sue. Money disappearing. Grace is scared because all her dreams for Lane's End are going down the drain."

Myra patted his shoulder. "Never mind, John. We are here now. The Vistas have arrived with bands playing and flags flying. . . ."

John interrupted her. "Up there, under the lamp post —see that group of kids near the truck? They are ours. I mean, they use the settlement. Everybody wave and look friendly, now!"

Patty couldn't make out any one person in the dark knot of young people. Everyone in the car waved, and Patty gave a toot on the horn to greet them.

Then, suddenly, there was confusion. A voice cried something Patty could not make out. The little group stirred and, in the dim light, seemed to change shape.

Before Patty could take in what was happening, a small body came away from the group and shot out into the street. "Right under the wheels," Patty thought, feeling a scream rising in her throat.

She threw the wheel sharp left and braked hard.

The car halted. Just as it did, she felt a dreadful bump under the front wheels.

CHAPTER 2

SOMETHING'S WRONG
AT LANE'S END

For a second Patty sat blind and still, not able to think
—not wanting to think.

Dimly she saw John under the lights of the car,
kneeling in the road.

"It's my fault," something far back in her mind repeated over and over. "My fault. If someone is . . .
hurt, it's my fault."

John was hidden now by a small crowd. It was terrible
—the silence, the grim yellow street light. Biting her lip,
Patty opened the car door. Then she heard John saying,
"It's all right—I think it's all right. Joe's quick as a
cat."

"He rolled away from the wheels." That was the voice
of a stranger. He turned toward the car, his face lighted
by a wide smile. "Too bad this had to happen." The
young man's voice carried a hint of Spanish in it. Hand-

some, well built, and better dressed than John, he certainly didn't look as if he belonged in this neighborhood. Yet he seemed to be in full command.

Patty wanted to get out and see for herself that the child was all right, but she couldn't seem to make herself move. He was already on his feet, a small Negro boy no more than ten, standing among his friends.

Then Ken was out of the car, facing the boy. "What's the idea, kid? What do you mean, running out in the street right in front of—"

That made Patty so angry she shot out of the car. The poor child, he might be hurt! And there was Ken chewing him out. That Ken!

Patty knelt down in front of the boy. "Are you sure you are all right?"

He glared at her. "Some terrible driver *you* are! I could be dead now this minute!"

"But is anything broken?" Patty asked. She remembered that awful bump. "I thought . . . something went under the wheels. . . ."

"Oh, my dirty old sneaker," Joe said, his eyes blazing. "I pull it off to hit some fresh kid, and you pick that minute to come whipping down—"

"Joe! I was doing less than fifteen miles an hour!" It was Patty's turn to get angry. "You know very well you almost jumped in front of me!"

Joe's friends started shoving and shouting. That made Patty nervous. She got up. "As long as you are okay," she said, and started back to the car. As she got in, she saw John talking to a policeman. Somebody called, "Hey, the cops!" And the little crowd broke up.

Suddenly Joe sneaked up to Patty. His eyes gleamed. "Psst," he whispered. "I jumped in front all right, but it wasn't my fault. Somebody *pushed* me. And it isn't *me* they are after!" He ran off quickly.

Patty got back in the car and started again. It hadn't been her fault, she thought as she drove along following John's directions. The boy had come leaping out under her wheels, and she had been lucky to stop in time. Why had he come up and whispered, "It isn't *me* they're after!" Who, then? Why? And who were "they?"

"Lane's End," John said beside her. Up ahead was what looked rather like a haunted house—lighted basement windows flickering from behind shrubs, a broad old-fashioned porch with a hanging lamp, deep windows on either side of the front door. The garage had once been a barn.

Patty looked quickly around her as they entered Lane's End House. Her family's little house back in Wisconsin was something like this, except that Lane's End had at least two of everything and was twice as big as any house she was used to. One front room had become a

library, lined with books. The other, filled with card tables and chairs, was used for meetings and classes.

But as Grace Pascoe came to greet them, Patty knew that she was very far from home indeed. This tall woman with sleek, gray hair and striking blue eyes was as different from Patty's small, soft-voiced mother as any woman could be. She gave each hand a firm, hard handshake as John introduced them and clicked off their names.

"Kenneth Smith. Myra Collins. Patty Mason." "Roll call," Patty thought. Their director was more like a general in the U. S. Army.

"You'll want to get squared away upstairs," she said in her deep voice. "John will show you—girls on the right, boys on the left. Then come down and we will put together something to eat and get acquainted."

Patty smiled and said, "I hope we will catch on to things soon." She was making small talk because no one was saying a word.

The woman frowned. "You've all had full Vista training, haven't you?" Her tone was stern.

Patty flushed. "Trained and ready for battle," Ken assured Grace, coming to Patty's rescue.

Grace smiled. "You'll have to forgive me for being jumpy. John may have told you we've been under a strain here lately, but I know it's all going to be better now you are here."

Ken smiled back. "You wouldn't be so sure if you had been with us in the car. . . ."

"Grace, what am I going to do about my busted glasses?" John broke in. Patty felt his elbow urging her toward the door. He kept on talking until the three others were half way up the stairs. Then he came leaping up to show them their rooms.

Lane's End had seen better days, and the rooms still

showed it. Patty and Myra each had a small room, both of them part of what had once been a large one. Patty's had a deep, old-fashioned window seat and Myra's had a fireplace. There was a tiny bathroom between.

Myra turned to John. "Back in New York they told us we would have to scratch for our own living quarters. I can't believe our luck!"

John nodded. "It's mostly Grace's doing. She talked everybody into letting us use this upstairs floor. She's got important friends everywhere that come kicking in with gymnasium equipment and the books downstairs and tickets to a ball game."

He got up and turned on Myra's small fan. "Let's get some air in here," he said. "You know, this place could do a lot of good. If Grace gives up . . ."

Patty glanced at him. "Was that the reason for the elbow treatment? You wanted us to shut up, but I didn't quite know why."

"The less trouble she knows about, the better," John said. "She is afraid that Lane's End is bad news around here. And it makes her touchier than ever with people, and that makes *them* touchier—well, you'll see."

Washed and combed, the girls went downstairs a few minutes later to find Ken helping to set the kitchen table. Chatting up in their rooms, they had decided that maybe Ken wasn't as bad as he had seemed on the train. He certainly knew when to smooth over things with a smile and an easy word.

It was a pleasant hour. Grace was friendly and talked of her early adventures as a church worker in Africa and China.

"Anything that wasn't a jungle village with mud huts seemed like high civilization," she said. "When the church social agency sent me here to put Lane's End on its feet, I was afraid it was going to be *too* easy."

John laughed. "She thought there wouldn't be any challenge. Shows how wrong you can be. She got off to a great start, then I came and . . ." He drew a finger across his throat and made a face.

"Nonsense. You are the best boys' director I ever worked with." Grace stirred her coffee as if she were mixing batter. "It's not you. It's this atmosphere that hangs over Lane's End. Something I can't put my finger on. Ah well, let's clean up and start breaking you people in."

It was heart breaking to look over Grace's early plans and see how they had fallen apart. She had set up wonderful classes for the local women, many of whom were newly arrived in the United States. There were classes in family planning, food buying, cooking with American food. At the beginning, large numbers of women had turned out.

"The first thing to go down the drain was the marketing class, but I welcomed that," Grace told them. "Some of our people got together and found out they could save a lot of food money by buying as a group. When you buy like that you get a much lower price. One of the local young men organized it—Guy Delvarga, who has been a great help to us. After that, the women didn't think they had much to learn about their food money." She frowned. "But then they stopped coming to everything else. Now it's . . ."

She paused as a motorcycle swept up the lane and came to a stop. "You think that's Ben Calder?" she said to John. "What's he doing here at this hour?"

There was a sharp rap at the back door and John opened it. Patty saw a heavy, bearded man who looked around with worried dark eyes. "Eddy's gone again," he said. "I guess he's not here this time, is he?"

"Oh no!" Grace spoke quietly. To Patty she sounded upset. "Gone again? I was so sure when I talked to him the last time he would stay put!"

John held the door wider. "Come on in, Ben. Ben Calder—our new Vistas." He made quick introductions. "How long has the boy been gone?"

Ben shook his head. Patty saw that his beard was actually short and neat—his strange appearance came from his long thick hair, which hung down over his shirt collar. He had a quiet, gentle voice and manner.

"Who knows?" he answered John. "I came across Millie—you know, his sister—running around looking for him. You know how she has felt about you lately. She will be here any minute, I would guess."

"Eddy O'Connell has run away four times so far," John explained. "His mother is in the hospital, and his sister is married to a guy who doesn't really want Eddy hanging around."

"Millie's husband isn't bad to him," Ben said. "At least he doesn't knock the kid around."

"What's that to be grateful for? That boy has a gift!" Grace said in an angry voice. "Those two can't make a plumber out of an artist! All they have to do is let him go to an art school instead of the trade school, and he would be an angel!"

Ben frowned. "Millie says Eddy never wanted to go there, until you started talking to him."

"He never *knew* about it!" Grace was dark red with anger. "It is part of my job to try to get kids off to the right start in life."

"How old is this boy?" Patty asked John softly.

"Going on fourteen." John turned to Ben. "Has she tried Father Dawson? The candy store? The Pizza Parlor?"

Before Ben could answer, a small, plump woman burst into the room. "You!" she screamed, shaking her finger under Grace's nose. "I told you to leave my brother alone! You had to go sticking your nose into our business, turning him against his own folks! If we ever find him, he will never come near this place again, you hear me? Or his friends either! Not if I have to go to the police!"

CHAPTER 3

AMALIA'S ALLEY

Everyone talked at once, and Grace looked ready to burst. Then she stalked out to the front hall, and some of the others followed.

"You are right—you are absolutely right," she muttered. "I must *not* lose my temper with that woman. But I talked to her till I was blue in the face about what would happen if she insisted on making Eddy learn what she calls a trade." She patted her damp forehead with a handkerchief. "Well, that's beside the point. The thing now is to find him."

After a quick council of war they decided to break up into search parties—John with Patty, Grace with Ken and Myra. As John and Patty set out, she felt he wasn't too worried. "Have you got any ideas?" she asked. John nodded.

The rain had stopped. It was pleasant enough going down Lane's End road, but when they turned into Main

Street with its old shops and houses, the damp heat rose from the pavement. The area was all gray, but Patty promised herself she would do something to improve it even if she taught just one child to read well!

John stopped in several stores and asked every young person they passed about Eddy O'Connell, but the answer was always the same: nobody had seen him.

"And they might not tell me if they had," John said. "They don't knock themselves out to help." He looked up the street to the bright sign that spelled out *Pizza Parlor.* "Might as well try there too."

Half the neighborhood seemed to be there, but Eddy wasn't in the crowd, and nobody had seen him.

"Okay," John said. "Now we can get down to business. Hang on."

They went on down Main Street. It got darker as they turned into an alley, lit only by a single lamp at the entrance. It was exactly the sort of place where you would be sure you heard foot steps following your own.

John's goal was a small shop whose window was blocked by a drawn curtain. On the glass was written in black paint: *Nature Cures.* John tried to peer around the edges of the door, when someone said behind them, "You think that crazy kid might be in here?"

Even as she whirled around, Patty knew who it was.

28

She recognized the musical voice. It was the young man who had been at the accident earlier that night.

"Oh, Guy." John stepped down from the doorway. "You get more like a cat every day. We didn't hear you come up." He turned to Patty. "You two already know each other, don't you?"

"Not the names," Guy said. "I'm Guy Delvarga."

"Patty Mason," she said. She had the crazy feeling that if they had been alone he would have kissed her hand. She could scarcely see his face, but the attractive build and pleasant voice reminded her of an actor in some foreign movie.

"He's very interesting," she thought. "He's very—exciting."

"How did you know about Eddy?" John wanted to know.

"How much goes on around here that I don't know about?" Guy asked. "You think he might be here with Amalia? She's locked up for the night."

John nodded. "Sure, but since she lives right behind the shop, what's to keep her from opening it for a friend? And she's got kids around all the time—as you know."

"Well, she won't open up for you. Look, why don't you two go round the corner and let me see what I can do. The boys know you don't want them hanging about here. . . ."

Patty followed John out of the alley and down the street. "Who's Amalia?" she burst out when they were away from the shop. "Come on, John—tell me!"

John leaned against a building, frowning. "Trouble is, we are not sure, Patty. Amalia's store has all kinds of herbs—you know, plants that are used for cooking and flavoring, like parsley and garlic and such."

"But you can get those in the grocery store," Patty said, disappointed.

"Ah. But what about a thing called bryonia, which is supposed to cure a cough? Or kalmia for a headache, instead of an aspirin? Or devil's shoestrings for teething babies—and evil spirits?" Satisfied with Patty's blank expression, John went on to explain that Amalia's shop was full of leaves, plants, and roots with even stranger names and uses.

"Medicines of this kind have been used all over the world for centuries. Some of them might even be better than the stuff we load ourselves up with these days. What we are worrying about is that Amalia might be selling other things that *are* dangerous."

"Like drugs? But can't the police . . ."

John shook his head. "The police have been here, believe me. They've never found a thing. Besides, the local women are all on Amalia's side. She makes up special things for them, for stomach aches and for having babies and for goodness knows what else—and it costs them pennies instead of what doctors charge. And it keeps them out of the hospital, which they all hate."

Foot steps came down the alley. Two sets of foot steps. In a moment, Guy appeared with a smaller figure behind him. "He found him!" Patty whispered.

John whispered back, "I think he knew all along where the boy was. He wasn't kidding when he said he's in on everything that goes on around here."

Eddy O'Connell was a very handsome boy, but his nasty manner could have easily got Patty's back up. Dropping beside him while John and Guy walked ahead, she tried to start a conversation. When she asked him if he had had anything to eat, he only shook his head. She couldn't keep herself from asking, "Would you like to tell me what it is all about, Eddy—I mean, the running away?"

That was a mistake, and she knew it right away. He looked up at her coldly and said, "You must be kidding."

Guy left them at the steps of Lane's End House. Grace and her search party had returned, and the local policeman had looked in. Ben Calder was still there too. That was fortunate, for as Eddy came in, his sister

Millie would have flown at him if Ben hadn't held her back.

"You rotten kid!" she shrilled, struggling in Ben's arms. "You want to kill me with worry!"

"Millie," Grace said, "shut up!" She spoke so loudly that she shocked Millie into silence. "I mean it. Eddy hasn't done anything that a thousand other boys aren't doing, and you are not to treat him like a criminal!"

Suddenly Millie sat down, covered her face, and burst into tears. Eddy turned his back on her, and to Patty's surprise he went over to Grace and talked to her in a low voice, all his bad manners gone. Perhaps Grace didn't do very well in dealing with older people, but evidently she knew her way with a boy like Eddy.

Patty exchanged a glance with Myra and Ken. "We can't help here," Ken murmured. "Shall we move on?"

Patty admitted to herself that Ken had a good point there. Both girls were more than willing to go to bed—they were so tired they were dead on their feet. But after she was ready for bed, Patty sat on her window seat and looked out into the quiet night. She saw Ben Calder pull away on his motorcycle. She must ask John how Ben fitted into the picture. A short time later, John, who must have found another pair of glasses, drove off with Eddy and his sister, taking them home.

It was almost 1 A.M., and Patty was now wide awake.

That was how she happened to see a familiar figure move out of the shadows near the house and go quickly and quietly down the road.

She lay in bed for a long time before sleep finally came. Too many things had happened in one evening. The boy she had almost hit . . . the new people she had met . . . the search for Eddy . . . and on top of all this, Guy Delvarga, the handsome young stranger, hurrying away from Lane's End at one in the morning— careful to go quietly so no one would see or hear him.

CHAPTER 4

OPEN HOUSE—AND AFTER

In spite of all the failures that made Grace Pascoe so unhappy, Lane's End was a busy place.

Three mornings each week, two teachers ran a school for two-, three-, and four-year-old children.

John, with Ken to help now, was either busy with one of the boys' sports clubs or out on neighborhood errands. He was visiting families of boys who had not shown up at the settlement house to see what was wrong. He was calling on local employers to drum up jobs or helping a family move when they couldn't afford hired trucks.

Myra began by teaching girls how to sew in a class in the club room. Patty became deeply involved with the work she had asked for—helping children with their reading problems.

For several days only two or three girls showed up— ten- to twelve-year-olds, shy at first, then slowly warming up to Patty. One day little Teresa Mendes, who had the biggest eyes and the longest braids Patty had ever seen, looked up from a word she had stumbled over and said, "That word was easy. It's only five letters. How come you don't yell when I miss easy words?"

"Because I'm here to help you. I'm not here to yell," Patty said.

"My sister yells. The teacher in school, she yells."

Patty leaned back and smiled. "What do you do when they yell?" she asked.

Teresa and the other girls looked at each other. "Quit listening," they said, almost with one voice.

They must have spread the word that Patty didn't yell, because bit by bit her group grew. A few boys showed up, little Joe among them. He was such a poor reader that Patty had to spend a lot of time with him, and one day she used the opportunity to ask him about the night of the accident. "When I almost hit you, Joe, remember? You told me something—"

"I don't know what you are talking about."

But Patty kept on, "Remember, you came to the car door . . ."

"Listen, are you going to help me read or should I cut out this minute?" the boy said in a furious whisper.

"Okay, Joe, forget it," Patty said. She had told no one about Joe's being "pushed." Now that she had seen Lane's End in broad daylight, and they had settled into

36

a working pattern, it was hard to remember that first strange night. Maybe Joe *had* been pushed—it could still have been an accident.

And yet . . . everything, everyone wasn't exactly what you'd call ordinary. There was that handsome Guy Delvarga, who seemed to appear when he was needed, disappear just as quietly when the trouble was over. And Ben Calder—it was true, as John had told her, that nobody knew where he came from or what he did for a living. But for Lane's End, he was a good thing. He was always on tap when help was needed. "It's like having two fairy god mothers," Patty thought, and then smiled to herself. No two people in the world could look less like fairy god mothers than Guy Delvarga and Ben Calder.

Actually, Ben was more of a mystery than Guy, Patty decided. Guy could be seen on the streets near Lane's End any day. But Ben—! When the trouble was over, he went off on his motorcycle—nobody knew exactly where —like a Robin Hood on wheels.

Patty caught her wandering mind and brought it back to Joe, who had been reading aloud a whole page, of which she hadn't heard one word.

Evenings, Grace Pascoe was often away from Lane's End. She was taking a course in Spanish at the state college, and she had many people to see and meetings to attend. John and Ken either organized games or walked around the neighborhood, keeping an eye on "their boys."

Much of the time Patty and Myra were left to themselves. A few nights of being alone were pleasant. But after a week they decided to get out, too, and find out what "their girls" were up to. Patty was especially eager to get a look at Nature Cures when the shop was open.

They found the alley without much trouble, and this Friday night it looked quite different—plenty of traffic, several of the shops still lighted.

"You must have really had the creeps that night," Myra said as she followed her friend down the alley. "Because this looks as lively as a county fair."

"Maybe Friday night makes the difference," Patty admitted. "But I tell you, Myra, there was something about it—and the way Guy suddenly appeared—"

"Sh-sh." Myra's hand closed on Patty's arm. Ahead, blocking the door to Amalia's shop, several big boys stood and stared at them. It was a street boy stare and it was meant to make them nervous, but Patty straightened and marched right at them. The shop was open —and she was going into it, whether those boys liked it or not.

Except for the dim lighting and the strange smells, Nature Cures seemed to be part candy store, part vegetable stall, part drug store. There were rows of big glass jars, labeled with names the girls did not recognize. Hanging from the ceiling were bunches of dried leaves and branches—all herbs, Patty imagined.

Over it all was a drift of cigarette smoke. When the door at the back opened, Patty realized the smoke was seeping in from the back room. Before the woman who came in closed it behind her, the girls caught a glimpse of young boys—under high-school age—sitting around, smoking.

"Can I help you?" the woman asked.

Patty didn't answer. She was busy sorting out her ideas. She had expected Amalia to look like a gypsy grandmother—old and wise and mysterious. The woman before her was tall and looked strong. In her smart striped dress, she looked about thirty. But her thick, long gray hair, drawn back into a heavy knot, added ten years. High cheek bones, a strong mouth, and dark, deep eyes . . . A shiver traveled up the back of Patty's neck.

"Was there something you wanted?" the woman said. "Or did you just come to see what you could find out?"

The boys who were still in the doorway laughed. Myra gasped. "What do you mean, find out?"

Patty stepped hard on her friend's foot. "That's *exactly*

why we came," she cut in with a bright smile. "I mean, we've been so curious about this place. We've never seen anything like it, you see, and we thought we would like to learn something about it. I hope you don't mind. We would like to buy some too."

"Some what?" asked the woman coldly. Patty was at a loss. "I have here perhaps a hundred different plants.

They all do something. Some cure, some make sickness, some make pleasure. Or pain." The hard, bright eyes seemed to soften. "Some have only a good smell. Perhaps some of those?"

"That's it," Patty said with relief. "Maybe some lavender? Or something else that smells good?"

The woman busied herself behind the counter, and handed out two little packets. "Lavender, rose leaves—and a little extra something to bring the future nearer," she said.

"Wow," Myra breathed finally, when they were on their way home.

Patty nodded. "She's a strange one all right, but not as queer as I thought. I expected her to be covered with beads and long earrings and other gypsy stuff. But all the same you certainly couldn't miss her in a crowd."

"You can say that again."

"What do you suppose she meant—it will bring the future nearer?" Patty wondered.

Myra shivered. "I would rather not know. I tell you, Patty, that place is poison. Did you see those kids in the back, smoking? At their age? They ought to be—"

Patty agreed. It would explain why the kids hung around there, though. If Amalia was encouraging cigarette smoking, why not other things?

Lane's End was lit up when they got back, as it

usually was. Grace kept it that way so people would feel free to drop in. But it was quiet and empty—too empty. Suddenly Patty said, "This is all wrong. If those kids are hanging out anywhere, it ought to be right here. Myra, we ought to have a party once a week!"

Patty's excitement was catching. By the time the others got in, the girls had a plan worked out for a dance the next Friday night. "It's such an obvious thing to do, I can't understand why it hasn't been done before," Patty said without thinking. Then she blushed. "Grace, I didn't mean to say anything against you!"

"Don't be silly, you are perfectly right." Grace got up and helped herself to coffee. "I thought of it, but I simply didn't feel up to it until you all came."

Ken was already making a list. "We will need music. We've got that old record player downstairs, and I guess we all brought some records with us. Say, maybe we can put together a little music group right out of the neighborhood. There's got to be some band around here. I can chase it down." Then he added, "If we can put it over it will look great on our Vista work records!"

"Oh, Ken," Myra said in disgust. "Don't you ever do anything except for the glory of Ken Smith and his work record?"

"What's the difference why I do it as long as it's a good thing to do? Look, I told you. If I come through this Vista year all right and the Army doesn't get me, my dad will help me go to Europe next summer—"

Myra clutched her short curls in despair. "Who *cares* about your trip to Europe? When you see how these kids live and how they have to struggle to get . . . to get even as far as the movies! You are the most awful—"

Grace Pascoe had sense enough to let the Vistas fight their own battles. John rapped on the table. "Time out, kids. Let's keep our eyes on the ball, please!" About twice a day he and Patty had to get between Myra and Ken to avoid a quarrel. Those two seemed to ruffle each other every time they so much as passed the butter.

Plans for the party went along well. John began to send out notices, and the others spoke to the people in their classes. Patty's young ones were so eager to come that she told them they could, if they would promise to leave at ten.

Food and soft drinks were the big problem. There was no money for this kind of extra. "And you can't have a party without Cokes and potato chips," Myra wailed. "We could run up some cup cakes out of a mix, I suppose, but we've got to have Cokes!"

"Let me try to handle that one," John promised. "Meanwhile, everyone down to the basement to decorate."

Decorating was a big word for the four rolls of crepe

paper they had squeezed out of their funds. Guy and a couple of his friends stopped by one evening and were not impressed by the results. But when they heard about the Coke problem, they disappeared and came back an hour later loaded with boxes of soft drink cans. "Not even bottles!" Grace exclaimed. "Nothing to break! Guy, you are magic."

"As long as we don't ask him how he did it," John said.

Guy grinned. "I promoted it. It wasn't hard. I went and asked in each grocery and each market. For the kids at Lane's End, I told them. Or else."

"Or else what?" John asked. Patty thought the look he gave Guy was rather sharp.

"My friend, I didn't really say that, you know. What do you think I am, a hold-up man?" Guy and his friends took the boxes upstairs to stow away in the huge ice box.

Patty was puzzled. Grace so often said that Guy, with his knowledge of the neighborhood and with his Spanish, was a great help. John seemed to feel the same way . . . but every now and then, like now, wasn't there a question in the way he looked at Guy?

She, herself, could find nothing wrong with anything Guy said or did. "There's something terribly exciting about him," she admitted to herself. "And it's not just

44

his looks, or that he's so different from everyone I've ever known. It's as if . . . oh, he had some extra strength or force in him that other people don't have. He's—he's like a thunder storm just before it breaks!"

The open house was a great success. Ken had found his little music group—a very good band indeed. The party went so well that the Vista girls had a bit of trouble gathering up the young ones at ten o'clock, but they made it.

The older kids danced their heads off, and all the food and drinks were gone by 10:30. But they still went on dancing. The one thing that might have spoiled the evening never happened. John told the girls afterward that while he was out driving the young ones home, a few tough older boys from outside the area had tried to crash the party. Ben Calder, who had "happened to be around" outside, hadn't cared for their manners or for the bottles of wine they had with them. Without bothering anyone, he had managed to get rid of them.

Patty was especially pleased that Grace's young friend Eddy had a good time. Eddy didn't come around very often. That night, he had put away his share of Cokes, and when he saw Patty he came over and said, "You people passed up a good thing. I could have painted

45

you a whole wall of pictures if you wanted. Better than this junky old crepe paper."

Patty stared at him. "Eddy! Now you tell me!"

"Well, you didn't ask me," Eddy said. "Next time speak up." He lost himself in the crowd, but he left Patty filled with excitement. They should have thought of it—getting the kids themselves to work for the success of the open house. Darting after Eddy, she shouted into his ear, "Come see me tomorrow. I want to talk to you."

At 11:30, when the party ended, there was no doubt in anyone's mind that the open house had been a great idea. The Vistas and John made quick work of cleaning up. In half an hour, "Dead End"—no longer quite so "dead"—was ready to call it a night.

They were about to go upstairs when Grace came out of her little office and said, "Come in for a minute, would you?"

She spoke quietly. Too quietly. Her hands were twisting in a way Patty had learned to watch for—a sign that her calm voice was hiding her real feelings.

"What's up?" John asked.

"You didn't go into my bottom drawer for anything, did you?" Grace's eyes swept over them all. "None of you? For any reason?"

They all shook their heads. The bottom drawer was where Grace kept cash on hand. It was locked. The money was in a locked box. The office, too, of course, had been locked. The windows at Lane's End had old-fashioned locks that really worked.

"Nothing has been broken into," Grace told them. "But there was more than 60 dollars in the box. And it's gone."

CHAPTER 5

PATTY MAKES A MISTAKE

"It's just not here." John sat back on his heels and gazed around the little office. They had all known that searching would do no good, but it put off for a while admitting the truth—that one of the open house guests had stolen the money.

"So here we go again," Grace said in a dull voice. She sat at her desk, tearing paper with nervous fingers and suddenly looking much older. "Things have been so much better this past week that I was beginning to have hopes."

John examined the desk drawer again. "We never missed this much before. I don't think this has anything to do with the other money we've missed. That was just peanuts, and we weren't always careful about locking it up. This looks to me like a different operation."

Ken put a pile of magazines back into the bookcase he had been going through. "My mother hides money away from herself in books," he explained. "Then she's very happy when she finds it." He went red. "I mean— of course if you had hidden it, Grace, you would have remembered. I just thought . . ."

". . . that I might be losing my memory?" Grace finished coldly. "Or losing my wits altogether? No—I don't think I'm that far gone."

Ken looked so hurt that Patty felt sorry for him. She said quickly, "When was the last time you missed money?"

John thought. "Three or four weeks ago. A couple of bucks. This looks to me as though someone had managed to get keys made to fit the locks—a real production." He looked at Grace. "Police?"

They were all surprised at the way Grace acted. "I won't have the police in here. The children will think they're being watched. Nor do I want the church board of directors to hear about it. We will try on our own to find out who took it."

"But that's like helping the thief," Myra protested. "Besides, don't we need the money for supplies and stuff?"

"The money is no problem." Grace spoke in her general's voice. "The real trouble starts if we get a lot of people in here telling us what we've done wrong." When Myra still looked bothered, she added, "You are very young, Myra, and it's hard for you to understand that one can't always go by the rules. Especially when you are dealing with people who do not live by the same rules you've been taught."

When they weren't too tired, the Vistas and John usually gathered for a late night talk in Patty's room. That night, Myra was still smarting from Grace's words. "Apart from everything else, doesn't it matter to her that Lane's End is out 60 dollars?" she demanded of John.

"Lane's End won't be out. She will do what she did the other times—put it back herself," John said. "Don't look so shocked. Grace isn't loaded, but she's got a little income apart from her salary—"

"And it's a lot better than letting the church board know that she isn't running Lane's End the way it ought to go," Ken put in. They all glared at him. "Look," he said, "you've got to admit it would look bad if people knew that kids she's been working with for months are stealing from her."

Patty was so angry that an absolutely crazy thought went through her head: *How much would an extra 60 dollars mean to that little fund of money Ken was saving up for Europe next year?*

When Eddy came over next morning to examine the basement wall and talk about painting it, he said the wall was in rotten shape but he would paint the picture if Patty still wanted one. "If you are going to have any more of these open house deals," he said, climbing a ladder to examine a bad crack near the ceiling.

Patty, holding the ladder for him, looked up. "Why shouldn't we? Didn't everyone have a good time?"

"Oh, sure. We just figured you wouldn't take a chance. I mean, you can't go on losing all that scratch every time you let anyone in."

Patty took a minute to cover up her surprise. "Scratch? You mean money. How did you . . . I mean, what makes you think . . ."

Eddy looked down at her. "Aw, come off it! The whole neighborhood knows the joint was knocked off last night. And quit shaking that ladder!"

"I am going to shake you off if you don't tell me what you are talking about!" Patty shook the ladder again and Eddy scrambled down. "Where did you hear it? From whom?"

But Eddy shook his head. He had said all he was going to say.

Patty didn't know what to do. Deep down, he was a lively, bright boy, just putting on a tough act. "Eddy, listen." She tried again, in a friendly voice. "You like Grace, don't you? And you know she thinks the world of you. If you could help her, you'd want to, wouldn't you?"

"And if you could make me squeal, you would, wouldn't you?" Eddy pushed his hands deep into the pockets of his torn jeans. "But you can't because I'm telling you the truth. I don't know where I heard it. Listen, do I do that wall or not? I've got to get over to my drug store job. I haven't got all day."

Patty gave up. Supplying him with paints from the store room, she left him and went up to the library in case anyone turned up for the reading group. A couple of girls came, and Teresa was among them. She was carrying something in a big paper bag, and she came straight to Patty and carefully took out a paper flower the size of a saucer. "For you," she said, her big eyes shy but eager. "For a present."

The flower was a beautiful arrangement of thin paper in shades of pink and rose, with a sparkling bead in the middle. "Teresa! Who made this?" Patty held it for the others to admire. "I've never seen such a lovely one. You didn't make it yourself, did you?"

Teresa was flushed with pride. "My mother, she makes them. At home we got hundreds. Bigger, even." She came close and lowered her voice. "My mother said, would you like some for the party? Next time, I mean.

I was telling her how the basement looked so—" She tried to find the right word.

"It looked poor," another girl said.

Teresa nodded. "So my mother said, if you would bring the paper she would make a lot. All colors. Big as a house, if you want."

Delighted, Patty asked the girl to stay after class. Grace was out, but John said that she had already put her own 60 dollars in place of the missing money and Patty could take a couple of dollars for supplies.

On the way to Teresa's they stopped at a little shop where Teresa said her mother got the fancy paper she needed. Then Patty and Teresa walked on toward the apartment building, each carrying a long, thin roll of beautiful tissue. In the brilliant sunlight even the shabby streets looked cheerful. As they passed the Pizza Parlor, Ben Calder was just getting off his motorcycle. He stopped to greet them.

"Bad luck about last night," he said. "Have the police turned up any leads?"

"Grace didn't call them in," Patty said without thinking. She bit her lip. "Please, Ben, forget I said that, will you? Grace doesn't want—"

"I didn't hear a thing." Patty still wasn't used to the strange contrast between Ben's wild appearance and his gentle voice. But his smile made her feel better. "I guess she's waiting for the good fairies to put the money back. She ought to know by now that it's not a good fairy that has her eye on Lane's End!"

Patty was troubled as she and Teresa went on. Ben was in and out and around Lane's End all the time. Nobody knew how he lived, or on what. Would 60 dollars be important enough to him . . . ?

She looked down as Teresa pulled at her arm. "That money. Did someone really take it? It's not just lost?"

"We think someone took it. It's nowhere at Lane's End, that's for sure." Patty stopped short. "You mean you know about it too? What did they do, put it on the midnight news?"

Teresa laughed. "Everybody knows about it! I bet plenty know who took it too!" She stopped laughing and threw a look over her shoulder. "Not me, though. How would I know a thing like that?"

Shading her eyes, Patty followed Teresa down paths lined with trees, past busy playgrounds and benches swarming with children, and into the small elevator of one of the project buildings.

A few days before, Patty had made a house visit with Myra, who had worried why one of her pupils hadn't come around for a while. That had been another kind of house, one of the broken-down frame ones.

The door had been opened by a little girl who looked

as if she hadn't washed for days. She had a cold, she explained in a hoarse voice. Her mother was out working. Yes, she was alone in the house—and she looked at the girls as if they had asked her something strange.

As they left, Patty and Myra almost tripped over a bag of garbage that someone had upset in front of the door. It smelled as if it had been there a long time.

"I wonder how long it will be before anyone cleans that up," Myra said as they reached the street.

"You mean, how long it will be before the garbage people pick it up, don't you?" Patty answered.

But the Mendes apartment was different. It was neat, the curtains were fresh, the few pieces of furniture were clean and shiny. Under a window, a large table was covered with paper and flowers like the one Teresa had brought, and the small woman who got up to greet them was clearly Teresa's mother.

Mrs. Mendes spoke little English. Patty beamed and nodded, stretching her few words of Spanish enough to make out what Teresa was explaining to her. Mrs. Mendes suddenly looked surprised. She replied in rapid Spanish. To Patty's ears, it sounded as though she was objecting to something. Patty began to feel very nervous.

"Teresa—" she began, putting a hand on the girl's shoulder. Teresa turned, her eyes full of tears. "Now what?" Patty thought. "What's going on?"

Just then the door opened and two people came in, laughing and talking. Patty found herself staring at one of the prettiest girls she had ever seen, her face framed in long, smooth dark hair. With her was Guy Delvarga.

The girl's eyes, even bigger than Teresa's, held a

curious look. Then, in a moment, the eyes were hard and cold.

Guy was the first to recover himself. "What a surprise!" he said to Patty. "You are learning very quickly to get around our neighborhood." He reached for the girl's hand. "Vicky, this is Miss Mason from Dead End House—I mean, Lane's End. This is Victoria, Teresa's sister."

Victoria bent her head without smiling and carried her shopping bag into the kitchen. Meanwhile, Mrs. Mendes and Teresa were speaking in angry Spanish to Guy.

Patty had never felt more strongly that she was in the wrong place at the wrong time. Perhaps she shouldn't have gone into the Mendes home without having arranged it ahead of time. But could that really explain the way Vicky Mendes had looked at her—almost with hate?

"Maybe," Patty thought, "she knows about me. Maybe Guy has talked to her about me. Maybe he's said such nice things about me that Vicky feels jealous."

Then she shook her head. "If Vicky's heard about me," she admitted sadly, "it's from Teresa. Guy hardly notices that I'm on earth." She smiled at her own foolishness. "If anyone's jealous, I am. I wish he'd look at me the way he was looking at Vicky as they came in."

CHAPTER 6

HELP!

It seemed that Teresa had offered the flowers without mentioning the fact to her mother. That was part of the trouble.

"It will work out," Guy said. "The problem is only that Mrs. Mendes must fill an order for a department store uptown—oh, yes, she does this work for money. When she has finished her order she will be glad to make flowers for the party."

"But we can't—" Patty began.

"She wants to. The mistake was that Terry did not tell her. By Friday morning you can have as many as you want. No, really," he insisted, as Patty tried to interrupt. "Vicky, tell Miss Mason your mother will do it gladly."

Vicky Mendes paid no attention to him. "But Mama must fill an order! This other thing—this is not important!"

Guy spoke to her in Spanish. Only a few quick words, but they made Vicky turn to Patty and say stiffly, "We are grateful to you for helping Teresa. She is reading better already. Mama will be happy to make flowers for the party."

"And now," Guy said cheerfully, "we offer lunch to your guest, Teresa!"

Patty remembered something John had impressed on the Vistas—the pride these people took in their treatment of visitors. "They have to know that you are a friend, not just someone handing out advice or charity but unwilling to give anything of yourself as a person."

Patty explained that Myra was waiting lunch for her. But, she said, she would love a cup of coffee. Teresa happily went with Vicky to prepare it. Guy explained that with Vicky's salary as a sales girl and the income from the flowers, the Mendeses were able to get along without welfare—something of which they were very proud.

"Not many families around here can do that," he said with a bitter note in his voice. "And I was able to help Mrs. Mendes find places that wanted her work. Vicky has ambition, and she is smart. Not many girls from this place can become sales ladies in such a high-class shop as she works in."

"She's so beautiful, I would think any place would

be glad to have her," Patty said. "But Guy—" She wanted to ask about Vicky's cold manner toward her, but the two girls came in with coffee and a plate of delicate rolled cookies Patty had never tasted before. Teresa said they were store bought—"just like plain old chocolate chip cookies. Only in a fancy box, with a funny name."

Patty was pleased when Guy insisted on leaving with her. But Victoria Mendes certainly didn't like it. At the door, the girl said, "Good-by, Miss Mason," so that it sounded like "Get lost!" Then she shut the door hard.

Her rude manner made it easy for Patty to ask Guy, as they walked through the project, what it was all about. "You are a good friend of the family," Patty said. "Vicky seems to trust you."

Guy glanced at her with the smile she had begun to watch for. "I hope so. We are—well, a little bit engaged. To be married."

Patty's heart sank. But she managed to say in a pleasant voice, "Guy, how nice! But what do you mean—a little bit?"

Guy picked up a ball and threw it back to a boy inside the playground they were passing. "Vicky has maybe too much ambition," he replied finally. "She wants more than anything not to be poor. And she is proud. She wants a husband she can show off—important, you know. With an important job. I work nights for a trucking company. I make a small amount of money on odd jobs. I am never sure she will be satisfied with me."

"I think you could do anything you put your mind to," Patty said. "I would bet my year's salary you've thought about college—"

"I've had one year—at night, of course. Not enough to lose my foreign way of speaking." Once again he spoke in a bitter voice.

Patty was surprised. "My goodness, is that so important?"

"You think it's not? To be put into a certain box every time you open your mouth? To be grouped with what you call *those people?*" Guy shook his head. "Maybe it's not impossible to get over this, but I have to make my mark a quicker way. My mark and my money."

"How, Guy?"

It was the wrong question. They crossed the street and as they passed what Patty had begun to think of as "Amalia's Alley," Guy said, "I go down here just now. But do not worry about Vicky."

"But why does she behave as if I were her enemy?" Patty asked.

Guy's eyes met hers with a gleam of laughter. She

was almost as tall as he was, and she suddenly remembered that Vicky Mendes came only to his shoulder.

"Are you so sure she has no reason to fear you?" he asked. "But don't worry. She will be more friendly. I think that may be your trouble. You are a girl who knows how to get people to talk. To some people, that makes you dangerous!"

Sunday night was staff meeting night at Lane's End, when they discussed the past week and planned for the coming one. But this time Patty didn't have her mind on it. What had Guy meant when he left her? She hadn't even talked about it with Myra, because Myra would have been sure to say, "He's very attractive. How do *you* feel about *him?*"

But when Guy had said she was dangerous, he wasn't flirting with her. He had meant something else. What?

As she described her visit to the Mendes house, Patty realized again how stupidly Terry Mendes had behaved, dragging her home like that. "And Terry's not stupid," she insisted. "Her reading is coming along beautifully. She's very sharp about a lot of things."

"Terry's hung up on you," Myra said. "Her best friend is in one of my classes—Kay Olvera—and Kay tells me she can't stand the way Terry talks about you all the time. 'Patty this and Patty that,'" Myra repeated.

Grace nodded. "It's simple enough. The most important thing for Teresa right now is to shine in your eyes."

"If Guy hadn't been there, I don't know how I would have come out of it," Patty said. "He certainly has a way with people. He even got Victoria to be polite—for a minute." Her cheeks started burning.

Ken smiled at her. "Could be that Terry and Guy have something in common when it comes to you, Patty. A couple of my boys were kidding about it at basketball practice last night. It would curl your hair if I repeated . . ."

"Why, I—" Patty stopped, because she could think of nothing to say that wouldn't give away how pleased she was. Guy *did* notice that she was on earth.

John came to Patty's rescue by rapping for silence. "Wasn't Vicky Mendes one of the girls who came to our job classes a few months ago?" he asked Grace. These job classes were one of their dead projects. After a good beginning, there had been so little interest that the talks about jobs had to be called off. "I would have run the whole class just for Vicky," John added.

Grace sighed. "I can shed some light on Vicky Mendes. She came into my office, the day after the first meeting to talk about it. I thought she was trying to find out when we were going to have someone over from one of the big department stores."

Grace flushed a deep red. "It turned out she was trying to say that *she* would like to talk to the girls. Most of them are afraid to look any higher than checking-out in the market or working as clerks in the five-and-ten. But Vicky has done better, and she thought she could offer some good advice, from her own experience."

Patty remembered what Guy had said about being "put into a box." Vicky, too, had been put into a box—by Grace. Grace had immediately taken her for someone who must learn and accept—not for someone who had something to give. By the time they got it straightened out, Vicky's pride was badly hurt. She had marched out and never returned. The chances were that she had warned all her friends against Lane's End too.

The school for the small children closed down that week for vacation, making it easier for Eddy O'Connell to work on what he called his "cave painting." He covered it up and wouldn't allow anyone to see it until he was ready. Meanwhile, Guy and his friends had promised to "promote" doughnuts, as well as soft drinks, for next Friday's open house.

Myra was all excited. She said that she had five new

64

girls in her sewing class and was starting to plan a fashion show for September. Things were looking up.

Patty tried once to talk to Terry Mendes about the paper flower trouble. She gave up quickly. The little girl could not understand that she had done anything wrong. "But Mama is making the flowers," she kept saying. "Don't you want them?"

"We are dying to get them! But don't you see you should have asked your mother first? You promised *her* time and *her* work, Terry, and you had no right—"

"But I work! I help her." Teresa's eyes were innocent, puzzled. "I hand her what she needs, I clean up. Vicky and me, we get the supper."

Patty sighed. Something else bothered her. Teresa seemed to be reading almost too well. Having in mind Grace's saying that Teresa was so eager to please, Patty started a system of follow-up tests. She was disappointed when she found that much of the time Teresa hadn't really understood at all. Words she seemed to recognize on Monday she could not recognize on Tuesday. It was discouraging.

On the other hand, there were the others, some of them doing very well. Little Joe, for instance, with the extra attention she gave him, had picked up greatly. But there was no more talk about who had pushed whom under the car that first night.

"Mama's got the flowers ready," Teresa reported when she came in on Thursday. "But it's like boxes full—" She spread her arms wide. "You better maybe bring the bus." She meant the station wagon, of course.

Nobody else needed it, so after a quick supper Patty drove it over. She was relieved that Vicky was out. Mrs. Mendes and Teresa were just finishing their meal, and she sat down with them to the usual coffee and a sort of salad, so delicious that Patty asked what it was. Hearts of palm, Terry told her, and Patty said she would look for it at the market.

The flowers more than filled the three large boxes she had brought. They were lovely. Patty's Spanish was picking up enough to know that the small, flushed woman was saying, "It was nothing. It gave me pleasure." At any rate, Teresa's pleasure and pride were easy to see. She stuck a blue flower behind her ear and fairly danced around Patty as they carried the boxes to the elevator.

Mrs. Mendes, nodding and smiling, was just closing her door when another door opened and a heavy, wild looking woman rushed out. "Mrs. Mendes, come look! Please—is very bad!" Her faded cotton robe fell open as she pulled Mrs. Mendes along with her.

"Boy! Tommy must be sick again," Teresa said. "I bet Mrs. Pinello wants me to go for Amalia again."

66

Patty's attention was sharp. "What's the matter with Tommy? Could we help?"

Mrs. Pinello's voice rose up in a scream. Quickly Teresa drew Patty into the Pinello apartment. The two women were in the living room with a small, fat boy, who was sitting in a chair. At first he didn't look as if he were in trouble. Then Patty saw that he was a very bad color, gasping for breath. Only the women were holding him upright.

Little Tommy was a very sick boy indeed.

CHAPTER 7

"NEW TROUBLE, VISTA?"

"Have you called an ambulance?" Patty demanded. "Is there a doctor in the building?"

Mrs. Pinello could no longer say a word. Mrs. Mendes spoke in rapid Spanish and Teresa said in English: "She called. They said, right away, but they're not here."

"You said he was sick before. Who's their doctor?"

"No doctor!" Mrs. Pinello said. "Go for Amalia, Terry! Go quick. She always knows—"

The boy's breathing came shorter and harder. Patty made a quick decision. "Get the elevator," she ordered Terry. "Hold the door open. Fast!" And she picked Tommy up. Tommy was heavy, and for once Patty was glad she wasn't a small, delicate female.

She never stopped to wonder how it was that Guy suddenly appeared before them in the downstairs hall. "Tommy is terribly sick!" she said. "I'm taking him to the hospital."

"Where's your car?" Guy wasted no words. When Patty told him, he said, "Take the elevator one flight up and go out the back—much faster. Go on. I'll start up the car."

A few more seconds, and Patty was placing Tommy gently across the laps of the two women, Mrs. Pinello shaking so much she could hardly hold on to him. In one hand she clutched a big lollipop and, to Patty's horror, she tried to push it between her son's dry lips. "He might choke!" Patty cried. "What are you doing?"

"Amalia said to give it to him when he's like this. It works. Last time it was good, you'll see!"

Only as she leaned forward in the seat did Patty realize that Guy was just sitting behind the wheel. The car wasn't running. He slipped out and pushed her into his place. "Keep trying. I can't get it started. I will go get a cab or something." He ran off.

With a helpless feeling, Patty turned the key and thumped the gas, but the engine would not catch. Teresa was close beside her, praying under her breath. Behind her Mrs. Pinello repeated over and over, "Why don't we go? He will die! You said you would take us!"

A small crowd of people was collecting. Someone called, "Hey, Vista, you got new trouble already?"

"There's Guy!" Terry suddenly cried. The crowd scattered as a police car whined to a stop in front of the station wagon. Guy got out, a policeman right behind him. In a few moments the car had taken off again, with the boy and his mother in the back.

Meanwhile Guy had fiddled around inside the engine and when Patty tried it again it was working. Guy got in with Mrs. Mendes and guided Patty to the hospital. When they went in, they found a nurse with Mrs. Pinello. Tommy had been taken upstairs.

As Mrs. Mendes hurried up to comfort her friend, Guy held Patty back. "I wouldn't talk to Mrs. Pinello just now. She's going to blame you—"

He was right. When the weeping woman looked up and saw Patty, her face grew dark with anger. "Why didn't you leave us alone?" she cried. "The doctor said the candy was right—Amalia was right! If I knew who you were I would never have let you touch my boy!"

"Don't look so shocked," Guy said to Patty. "Every time she has anything to do with Lane's End it brings her trouble. She just wants to stay away from you."

Patty was so angry she didn't know what to say. But she had to find out how Tommy was, and when a young doctor came down and started questioning Mrs. Pinello, she drew near enough to hear them. The boy was all right, evidently, but the doctor wanted to know some things Mrs. Pinello couldn't seem to tell him. He turned to Guy. "Ask her who's been taking care of the boy," he said.

"She doesn't have a doctor," Guy told him. "She just goes to the herb shop."

"Oh no!" the doctor groaned. "Not Amalia again! Good lord, man, the child has diabetes! He was in a very bad way when we got him!"

Patty stared, not able to speak. And they took him to Amalia for such a serious illness? "He could have died," she said.

The doctor studied the information the nurse had handed him. "Maybe this is the first serious attack he's had. With a kid it can sneak along for a while and not hit hard until he eats something wrong or exercises in some unusual way. And besides, chances are she would have gone to Amalia anyway. The faith that woman creates is remarkable."

"She is cheap too," Guy said. "And they don't have to come to the hospital and wait six hours till someone is free to see them." The doctor flushed.

Patty remembered the lollipop and asked him about it. Mrs. Pinello had been telling the truth: the candy *was* right. "It's exactly what we are doing," the doctor explained. "A big lift of sugar is what he needed. The lollipop would have worked if he hadn't been so far gone. That's where Amalia has us every time we get a patient who's been going to her. She knows the right thing to do—up to a point, at least. Some day when I retire I'm going to look into plant and herb medicines."

Patty didn't get much sleep that night. The doctor had put a strange idea into her head. A wonderful idea. "But Grace will never go for it," she thought as she finally dropped off.

It still seemed like a good idea next morning. But with open house coming up, it would have to wait. Guy had brought over some doughnuts and reported that the rest would be there later. Money had somehow been squeezed out of the funds for a few new records.

At 4:30, Eddy had to leave for his drug store job. Opening the basement door a crack, he let Patty and Myra squeeze in for a look at his painting. "But it's not really finished," he warned.

Patty had expected Eddy's painting to be good, but she was truly surprised even so. He had done a view of the whole neighborhood, not like a photograph but in a style of his own, with small brilliant blocks of color that came out like a stained-glass church window. As they looked they began to pick out familiar things: project buildings, Main Street traffic, Amalia's Alley—everything that was important to Eddy.

Nobody heard Guy come in. "It's really great, Eddy," he said.

Eddy gave a sigh of relief. Praise from the girls had pleased him, but praise from Guy was more important. He went off in a cloud of happiness.

When the beautiful big flowers were up, the basement looked bright and gay. Grace, just returned from a day "uptown"—which meant another effort to raise money —brought back a pleasant older man named Gilbert Nelson. He was one of the church board officials who watched over Lane's End. The gay decorations and the feeling of a party in the air seemed to please Mr. Nelson. "Things look really lively," the girls heard him say as John took him upstairs. "Really go-ahead. I will be anxious to see . . ." They couldn't catch the rest.

Grace's eyes were bright with hope. "I'm so glad you had this done in time for him to see it! He's been my biggest trouble, as far as getting money goes. That's why I dragged him down tonight. When he sees what we can make of these open house nights with just a little more money, even he won't be able to say no."

"I wish she hadn't said that," Patty wailed after Grace had gone. "Something's *bound* to happen now!"

In a way, she was wrong. Nothing happened. Really nothing. Almost nobody came.

By nine o'clock, only a handful of the younger kids had shown up, and the music pounded out to an empty dance floor. At 9:30, they gave up and John and Ken drove the young ones home. Myra and Patty tried to get past the closed door of Grace's office without her hearing them. She hadn't come down after Mr. Nelson drove off, and the girls had a strong feeling she was in there crying.

But she called out and they had to go in. If Grace had been crying, all trace of it had been wiped out by anger. She had evidently been arguing with Ben Calder, who sat with folded arms, looking like a man with his mind very much made up. Grace said, "Ben could have told us hours ago it was going to be a complete flop."

"What good would it have done?" Ben said mildly. "There was always a chance some of them would show." The girls were silent, waiting for an explanation. "All I know is, a lot of kids came up to me and asked if I thought there might be police around here tonight on the account of the money that disappeared last week."

Grace snapped a pencil in two. "How *do* these stories get around? When I made such a point of not telling the police a word—"

"Come on, Grace, every kid in the neighborhood knew!" Ben picked up the heavy leather gloves that he was never without. "You bet your life there were going to be extra police around tonight. And you know as well as I do that plenty of the older boys are already better known to the cops than they want to be. It made good sense for them to stay away."

Myra said, "Why, that sounds as if you told them not to come!"

"Why not?" Ben said. "They asked for my opinion and I gave it to them. They are my friends."

"But—we thought you were on our side!" Grace said exactly what Patty was thinking.

"I'm not on any side," Ben said flatly. "That's your big problem, Grace. You on one side, the neighborhood on the other, and you fighting to pull them over. I don't believe in taking sides. When I see some way to help a friend, I do it. I thought police might be watching over some of the boys too closely, so I told them."

Catching sight of John and Ken coming in, he broke off and grinned. "Anyway, if I've upset anyone, I'm sorry."

"Who was it said with friends like him who needs enemies?" Ken asked, when Ben had gone and he and John had been filled in on the discussion. "More important, what are we going to do to get the customers back for next Friday night?"

"I wouldn't give that much thought," Grace said. "Funds can be cut as well as increased. We might have to cut down on everything."

Her hands started twisting together. "I didn't want to

tell you this, but the church office has been getting letters about us. Letters signed with false names, not one that I recognized. They say Lane's End is a bad influence down here. They say we are making trouble."

CHAPTER 8

PATTY TAKES ACTION

"What this amounts to," Ken said, "is that someone doesn't want Lane's End around here."

It was after the staff meeting on Sunday night. Grace had heard nothing from Mr. Nelson, but the gloom was as heavy as though the ax that would chop the funds had already fallen.

It was crazy. Lane's End was breaking its neck to do the neighborhood good. Who would want to stop them?

Ken had an answer. He thought it was because of Grace.

"The kids we've been working up into a basketball team call her the queen. She's someone not from their world. As Ben said, she's on one side and they are on the other."

"Hog wash," John said in an angry voice. "We should have one-tenth of her know-how with this kind of work!"

78

"Sure—in Africa, maybe in India. But these people down here are just as much Americans as she is.

"I know"—Ken held up his hand as Myra started to speak—"you think I have the same outlook—that I'm better than they are. Maybe I did have it once and that makes it easier for me to see where Grace goes wrong. Myra has made a lot of house calls. Some of her girls have become very friendly. John and I eat over in the Pizza Parlor a couple of times a week, and always with a gang of boys."

He turned to Patty. "You've had coffee with the Mendes family. Who feels comfortable enough with Grace to ask her to sit down at their table?"

"Coffee, nothing. Hearts of palm salad," Patty put in. "That puts me one up on the rest of you. I *really* got to eat what the family was eating."

Ken was surprised. "You don't mean hearts of palm. Do you know what that stuff costs? Hearts of palm costs around a dollar a can. When my mother is having some fancy people for dinner she gets stuff like that."

"Oh, we all know you could give us lessons in the good life," Myra snapped. "Maybe there's more than one kind of this stuff, cheaper. Maybe you don't know absolutely *everything*—"

"And maybe there's a reason why the Mendes family

can have little extras like dollar-a-can food," Ken flashed back. "*Someone* has been taking that money!"

Up in her room, Patty was restless. Suppose, that first night, little Joe had meant what he had whispered? Suppose Eddy's sister had written those letters about Lane's End bringing trouble? That woman hated Grace. Ben Calder—was he a friend? Ben Calder, picking up those black gloves . . . why gloves in this weather? Finger prints? Ben was in and out all the time. He could easily have had keys made to fit every lock in the place. . . .

After the Friday night flop, it was a surprise when almost everyone showed up for Monday classes. Ben might have had the right answer: the missing money had been connected with open house, and it was only open house that the kids had stayed away from. Patty caught herself watching Teresa with unusual attention. After class she held the girl back, without knowing exactly what she was going to say. Then she remembered to ask about Tommy Pinello.

"He's okay," Teresa said. "But his mother, she's supposed to have a doctor now and not Amalia any more. Amalia will be chewing nails. She curses like anything when people go to doctors instead of her!"

"Does your mother go to Amalia for medicine?" Patty asked.

"Well, sure!" Teresa's eyes opened wide at the foolish question. "She gave us something to make me smarter in school. And—" She laughed. "She gave Vicky something to make Guy like her better."

Patty had a sudden idea. "Teresa, do you think Amalia might have told the older ladies, like your mother and Mrs. Pinello, not to come to Grace's classes? Like maybe she was afraid we would tell them to go to doctors and not to her when they were sick?"

Teresa backed toward the door. "I don't know anything," she said quickly. She jumped like a frightened rabbit as she backed into Guy, who was just coming in. Then she turned and ran.

Guy laughed. "I didn't think I was so bad I scared children. Look, I came to see if you want me to get rid of all those doughnuts and things you did not use."

Patty said she was sure they could manage—and then wished she could take the words back, because Guy, with a smile, turned and left.

"If I'd kept him here, I could have asked him questions," she told herself. And then she admitted the real reason: "And besides, I *wanted* him to stay. It would have been fun just to talk to him."

But then, she told herself, Guy wasn't one to "just

81

talk." Everything he said seemed to have meaning and purpose—if only the person listening could understand!

"Anyway, what questions could I have asked him?" she comforted herself. She had heard him come to Amalia's defense. She could hardly ask him if Amalia might really have given Vicky something to make him fall in love with her, or Teresa something to make her smarter. A drug—to a child of 11?

That night Patty went to the public library and took out a book called *Plant Medicine Through the Ages*. Besides the chapters on plants used as medicines there was a chapter on "black magic" plants—not the common drugs that could be read about in the papers every day, but unusual ones that the police would not know enough about to look for.

Was it because she had plants like these that Amalia didn't want anyone from the outside coming around to check on her?

There was one way to find out. And it was a way that might kill an even more important bird with the same stone. She would have to try out the idea she had had the other night—the far-out idea that the doctor, without knowing, had put into her head. And that meant braving Nature Cures once more.

Patty would have asked one of the others to come along, but that evening Myra was typing for Grace and the boys were head deep in the engine of the station wagon, which had been going poorly ever since the night of Tommy Pinello's illness. So she took *Plant Medicine* in one hand and her courage in the other and set off alone. The alley was empty, but Nature Cures was lit up, the door open. As Patty entered, two girls about her own age were leaving.

It was hard to begin under Amalia's cool, dark eyes. Patty put the book on the counter. "I've been reading this," she said. "It's about" —she waved at the room— "the stuff you sell. It's interesting."

Amalia glanced at the book. "Yes?" That was all she said.

"Well, I—got interested. I wondered if—"

"I know what you wondered." For the first time, Amalia showed a feeling: anger. She glared at Patty. "You wondered what dirty tricks I am up to in my dirty little shop. Just like the police have wondered. Well, you will find what they find. I do not give the children bad things. I do not sell them drugs that will poison them."

She drew a deep breath. "The police have been here four, five times, and they never have found anything wrong. They never will, because I do not have anything wrong!"

"You don't understand," said Patty. She was making

a mess of this, she was afraid, but she had to go on.
"That's not why I came at all. Listen, Amalia," she
pleaded. "The other night a little boy named Tommy
Pinello had to go to the hospital—"

Amalia nodded with satisfaction. "Yes—and the doctor
said that the candy I told his mother to give him was
right, is that not so?"

"Yes," said Patty eagerly. She had given up wondering how news got around the way it did. "There's a lot in this book about how regular doctors are getting interested in your kind of medicine."

Amalia's eyebrows went up. "That is so?"

Patty fumbled for the right words. "Your cures are not really looked down on by doctors. Maybe people should know more about them. So—so I thought maybe you would consider coming to Lane's End once a week and giving a talk about your plants and herbs."

For once, Amalia lost her stony look. "You want me to give lectures?"

Patty nodded. "Yes—and I'd like to listen to them too. I'd like to know more about nature cures."

"There is much to know. I would have much to say." Amalia spoke slowly, as if talking to herself. Then, for the first time, she smiled.

"From early times, herb doctors have been known— and respected—in every country of the world. In many places, especially on islands where there is still little known of modern ways, herb doctors are still powerful and thought much of." Her eyes had a strange look in them, Patty noticed—as if in her mind she were seeing those far away places.

"I, myself, come from the island of Haiti," Amalia went on. "There for many years my ancestors have been herb doctors, far back in the hill country." Now the smile had mischief in it. "You think I am a white woman, no? That is not so. Some of my ancestors were white, but some came from Africa, long ago." She sighed. "Yes, I would have much to talk about at Lane's End."

Suddenly there was a scraping noise from the back room, and Patty's heart sank. If she so much as looked curious, Amalia's mood might change. She might throw her out. She might decide against giving the lectures.

But Amalia opened the back door and said a few words to whoever was inside. Then she came back. "Those boys who like to come around," she said quickly, "—it is nothing bad, you know. Here they can smoke and their mothers do not yell at them. If they smoke a little at this age, maybe they will not want to later. And they play cards and think they are big men." She studied Patty's face to see if she understood.

"They would do it anyway, Amalia," Patty said.

"Yes," Amalia agreed. "And better here than on the street." She was silent for a minute. "Tell me when and I will come."

Patty walked on air through the alley and down Main Street. Her first truly independent operation, and it looked like a success! It looked as though she had turned an enemy into a possible friend for the settlement!

Only . . . what would Grace say?

86

Patty decided to return the book to the library before going home to face Grace. As she passed the Pizza Parlor some young men came out, Guy among them. He called to her to wait and then fell into step beside her.

"Buy you a cup of coffee?" he offered.

Patty explained about getting to the library before it closed, and Guy nodded. "The offer is good after nine. You haven't seen much of our bright night life around here—like at the Pizza Parlor."

Patty laughed. "Even the Pizza Parlor might go to my head after a hard day's work."

"I see," Guy said stiffly. He had put a hand on her elbow as they crossed the street, now he drew it back. Patty realized she had made a mistake. "But I will risk it," she added.

The place was jammed as always, and everyone greeted Guy and took a long, hard look at her. She was remembering what a big thing Ken's boys had made out of seeing her with Guy. "What will they make of this?" she wondered, smiling to herself. "Plenty—I hope!"

The Pizza Parlor was lively. Guy was an attractive young man . . . and he seemed to think she was attractive too. Patty enjoyed herself very much. She wasn't a Vista worker exploring the neighborhood with a native. She was a girl on a date, and she hoped Guy thought of it that way too.

As they walked toward home she found herself telling Guy about Amalia. "I shouldn't say a word until Grace okays it, but wouldn't it be wonderful?" she said. "Instead of always bringing in outside people to give talks —to have someone everybody knows and already respects?"

Guy didn't reply at once. "Don't you think it will work?" Patty asked him. "Won't they come?"

"Oh yes. They will come," Guy said quietly. "It will show that one of our own can be important enough to stand in front and give advice and information."

At the foot of the Lane's End steps he stood looking at her thoughtfully. "You are a very smart girl, Patty. Around here it is sometimes better not to be so smart. . . ."

CHAPTER 9

GIRL MISSING!

"All right," Patty said to herself in the mirror next morning as she brushed her hair. "What did he mean by that one?"

She had gone to sleep with the same question—Guy was always leaving her with a question.

She was frowning as she ran down for breakfast. The atmosphere had changed last night, after she had told him about Amalia. Changed in a way she couldn't put her finger on. And what had he meant by that last— was it a warning?

She was just finishing when John came down. "I need information from you," he said, sitting down. "What exactly happened the other day when the car wouldn't start? The spark plugs are all wrong."

Patty told him again. John frowned.

"One of the sparks looked as if it had been half pulled off. I never heard of that happening by accident.

Pity it had to happen in front of a whole mob. To them, I guess, it was another Lane's End foul-up."

"True," Patty thought, remembering the laughter of the people standing around. But maybe with Amalia they could start fighting back, changing the Dead End image. She tried out her idea on John. He was sure Grace would be crazy about it.

When Grace came back, Patty felt encouraged enough to tell her about it immediately. John had been wrong. She wasn't crazy about the idea. "These people need the best advice and information they can get," she said. "We owe it to them."

"But it's such a special subject," Patty urged. "And they have so much faith in Amalia. My idea was that they would be proud that we thought someone who is . . . well, sort of their own rather than ours, and important enough to be set up in front of them, more like our own experts."

Grace frowned. "That's another thing. Can she handle it—talk well enough?"

"She comes on like Elizabeth Taylor and Richard Burton put together," Patty said eagerly.

In the end, Grace said yes.

Nothing could be done that day, for they were all busy setting up the basement for a basketball game that Ken and John were hoping would draw a big crowd.

The basement had to be cleared of the open house decorations and chairs set up against the walls. Because Grace's office could be locked, they carefully piled the paper flowers on her desk, chair, window ledge, and in the corners. But at least Eddy's painting still blazed across one wall of the basement.

The game was a fair success. Looking over the small, but not too small, crowd, Patty thought it contained a surprising number of younger kids. Teresa and her friend Kay Olvera were there, little Joe, and others she knew. But not many were as old as the boys on the teams. The players couldn't have cared less. Ken's team won 60–57, but all of them played their hearts out.

The game was over early, and the Lane's End staff felt much more cheerful as they went about locking up. Patty and John were standing at the window when suddenly a small dark car drove up. Two people got out— Guy and a girl. "Vicky Mendes!" Patty peered again to make sure. "What do you suppose—at this hour?"

Vicky came in stiff and silent, and Patty suddenly realized the girl was not only angry but frightened as well. Guy explained, "It's Teresa. We know all the others are home, and we wondered if there was some reason why she is not."

It was more than an hour since the place had cleared

out. Grace said, "How can she not be home? Unless she stopped somewhere. The Pizza Parlor?"

Vicky turned on her. "She has not stopped. She has strict orders when to be home, and she follows them. We know how to raise our young ones—maybe better than you do!"

Guy and Vicky had checked all of Teresa's friends, Amalia's, any place they could think of. Patty fought down fear. Somehow she was certain that Teresa would not turn up bouncing and smiling from some place they hadn't thought of. Something had happened to her.

Twenty minutes later the Vistas were sure she wasn't anywhere in Lane's End. With six of them to cover the place from attic to basement, it didn't seem possible that they could have missed any corner.

With his sure feeling for trouble, Ben Calder arrived as they were trying to decide if it was time to call the police. "Saw the place lit up, saw the car, knew something was up," he explained. When they told him, he said, "Of course you've got to call the police, right away. The kid's 11 years old and small. She could be picked up in one hand."

"Oh, don't!" Patty begged, glad that Vicky was at the other end of the hall. "Ben, what can we do?"

"Get the police, then gather up all the flash lights you've got and we will go over the lane from here to

Main Street. It's only a short distance, but it's very dark and the trees and bushes are heavy enough to—" He saw that Patty was biting her lip and finished, "Anyway, it's got to be done."

It was done, with no result. The police car arrived as they were combing the bushes, and the police joined them with their powerful lights. When they were finished they knew that at least Teresa was not a limp little bundle lying hidden under the Lane's End bushes.

But there were other places. Other things that could have happened. Things that didn't bear thinking about. . . .

The search for Terry Mendes went on through the night. Mrs. Mendes had been asleep when Vicky first became worried. But of course there was no way to keep it from her forever. Patty was surprised at the way she took it. No tears, no wringing of hands. The thin little woman simply turned to stone, holding in all the terrible fear she must be feeling.

The Vistas, of course, wanted to keep on searching, but Lane's End had to be kept going. Patty rested for an hour on her bed without getting into it, then got up, showered, and put herself together for the day. She was too keyed up to be tired, but from the way she kept dropping things she knew she was hardly at her best.

She lost and found her hairbrush twice, and spent five minutes looking for the bottle of perfume her mother had given her as a going-away present—a bottle that she always put back in exactly the same spot on her dresser because it covered a stain in the wood. It was on the floor beside her bed, and her head ached so much she couldn't remember how it got there.

From the looks of the others, they were all in the same shape. But Myra and Patty met their classes as always. They tried, without frightening the children, to find out if any of them had the least bit of information. Of course everyone in the neighborhood knew Terry was missing. Still, the Vistas tried to give the impression that nobody was really worried.

"Of course nobody's worried," Myra said bitterly when

she and Patty met in the kitchen at noon. "Little 11-year-olds are always staying away from home all night—and in a poor section of town too. Who's worried?"

Kay Olvera had not been in class, so they hadn't talked to her. But the police had seen her and her parents the night before, with no result.

"They are down to cellars and locked-up stores," Ken reported when he came in. He and John had spent the morning with the police, hoping they might get help from boys who would freeze up under questioning by police men. He shook his head at the offer of a sandwich. "If only there were something to go on. If only she had ever said anything about running away."

"She never carried more than a dime in her pocket that I know of," Patty said, trying to be practical.

Ken came to a halt like a bird dog. "What if she had more than a dime? Where's Grace? We've got to find out if anything is missing!"

"Ken, you really are a rat—" Myra began furiously, but Ken was gone. Myra turned to Patty. "You know what he wants? He's not worried about Terry! He wants his picture in the papers—*Ken Smith, Vista worker, clears up girl's disappearance.*"

Patty got up and poured her a glass of cold juice. "Calm down, Myra. Ken is not such a bad guy. The way you blow your cool over him, sometimes I wonder

95

if you aren't just trying too hard to convince yourself you can't stand him." She spoke without thinking, her thoughts really on Terry. She was surprised when Myra turned bright red and ran out of the room.

Patty stared after her. What had she said to throw Myra like that? Something about Ken—about convincing herself she couldn't stand him. But if a thing was true, you didn't have to convince yourself that hard, did you?

"How thick can I be?" Patty wondered. "How could I be practically living in Myra's pocket and take this long to see how she really feels about Ken?"

At that moment Grace's office door opened, and she and Ken came into the kitchen looking sick.

"In one way it's almost a relief," Grace was saying. "At least she wasn't kidnaped. She's gone of her own free will."

Patty froze. Ken said, "Grace cashed a two-hundred-dollar check yesterday and put the money in the box in her desk. Even the box is gone this time."

CHAPTER 10

ANOTHER BLOW FOR GRACE

The worst of it was, not even Patty—who knew Terry best—could say, "Terry would never steal!"

Terry's sense of right and wrong was very much her own. So eager to please, she didn't always tell the truth. "And there were a dozen ways," Patty thought, "in which Terry might persuade herself to take the money and not think of it as stealing."

Yes, Terry could have taken the money. One reason that made Patty sure was that the paper flowers in Grace's office had not been crushed. They had been carefully moved aside so that the thief could get to the desk.

But, being Terry, perhaps, instead of persuading herself, she had *been* persuaded. Patty hung on to that thought as the search went on. She kept telling Myra, "They'll find her. She will have taken the money—but it will be for a reason we can't begin to imagine."

The police talked again to little Kay Olvera, certain that no 11-year-old would be able to carry off such an adventure without telling her best friend. In the end, they did find out something. "I know she's all right," Kay said through her sobs. "I don't know anything, but I know she's all right." But they couldn't get any further with her.

By late afternoon even Patty, who always had more energy than she could use up, was dreaming of dropping down on her bed for just a few moments. She finally managed it. No sooner was she down, though, than she had to get up to answer a soft knock on her door.

No one was there. Puzzled, she went back to bed, stumbling over a shoe on her way. Picking it up to put it back with its mate on the window seat, Patty suddenly remembered that she had put both shoes on the window seat together. She seldom left clothes around. For a teen-age girl she was almost too tidy. But she remembered thinking, "I ought to put these in the closet, but I'm just too tired."

Patty stared at the window seat. It was just a window seat, the top padded for comfort. She had never noticed how big it was. As she stood there, the soft thud came again—but not from the door.

Her heart jumped and her lips were dry as she put

her hand on the window seat top. If it moved . . . if it came up . . . *It came up.*

Patty looked down into what amounted to a deep, high box—and found herself staring into Terry Mendes' face, smiling though wet with tears.

She scarcely took time to help Terry out before she ran for the phone: it was important to save Mrs. Mendes any further worry. Then she ran back and dragged Terry into the bathroom to wash while she shot out a rapid fire of questions.

"I'm too hungry," Terry said. "How can I answer when I'm starving? I had peanut butter sandwiches and cookies but they only lasted like ten minutes!"

Patty ran downstairs again and grabbed some food from the ice box. She had to get Terry's story before anyone else.

Terry was more than willing to talk. And at the end of ten minutes Patty knew . . . nothing. "The money's all there," Terry kept saying. "I had it with me—the box and everything. I didn't take any."

The box was still locked. "I can see you didn't take any," Patty said sharply. "I'm asking what happened. Why did you do any of this?"

"I just thought of it," Terry said. "I thought I'd take the money and disappear and then . . ." She stopped. "I can't remember."

"You mean—like you had a loss of memory?"

"I could have." Terry's large eyes were as clear as ever. "It was hotter than—it was hot in there. I kept coming out every time you went out of the room and jumping back in when I heard you coming. Are you mad because I took your perfume? I didn't use much." She laughed. "How come you didn't find me?"

She talked on, and Patty felt a sense of defeat. She was sure Terry was chattering like this on purpose because she wasn't really going to tell anything like the truth.

Finally she asked, "What were you planning to do? How long were you going to stay in there?"

For the first time Terry's face clouded. "I don't know. I wasn't supposed to be there at all. I was supposed—" She clapped a hand over her mouth.

Patty pulled it away. "Terry! Did somebody put you up to this? Tell me!"

But Terry only shook her head.

There was noise downstairs—people hurrying in. Defeated, Patty took Terry down and turned her over to her family.

Nobody got anything more out of Terry. She stuck to her story that she "didn't remember." And since the money was safe, the police decided she was just a crazy kid who had been looking for attention, and they let her go.

Without fuss, Grace and John managed to get her over to the hospital where a doctor talked to her, trying to find out if Terry might possibly be what was politely called "disturbed"—not quite normal.

"Sharp as a tack in some areas, absolutely average-normal in others," the doctor said. "She's lying, that's all. She may have been scared or threatened into it, but she's not in a state of terror. Leave her alone and forget it. There's been no harm done."

The person really harmed was Grace. Under the eyes of the others she simply began to come apart. A few days after things had calmed down, she was called to a church board meeting from which she returned in tears. They had had her on the carpet about the whole Lane's End picture, in which Terry might just be the last straw.

"They're one step short of deciding we are more trouble than we are worth," she reported. "The letters, the breaking down of the program, and now this. It looks to them as though we encourage the kids to do these crazy things. As for more money"—she waved her hands about—"forget it. We will be lucky if we keep operating."

Strangely, Grace's despair didn't rub off on the others. It had the opposite effect. After Grace had gone to bed, they talked it over and agreed that what they wanted to do was fight back.

"Have the open house! Let Patty set up Amalia's talks! Let Myra's girls go on with the fashion show!" John pounded his fist with each item. "What have we got to lose?"

They decided to go all out on the next Friday night—a basketball game with an open house to follow. The girls had to do most of the work themselves, for Ken and John were also building up their job program, calling on business men all over town to drum up job chances for more of their boys. A boy with a good part-time job was more likely to be a boy who went back to school in September.

Patty, trying to get hold of Guy for food and soft drinks, found that nobody knew where Guy lived—or nobody would say. In the end, she left a message for him at the Pizza Parlor, and she wasn't surprised when Ken said his team had started kidding again about her and Guy.

"I'd lay off, Patty," he advised. "Of course we all know you couldn't be interested in a guy like that—but still—"

"And why couldn't I?" Patty challenged. There was Ken, looking down his nose again!

"You mean you *are* interested?" he said, surprised.

"I mean you shouldn't be a Vista with that upper-class attitude!"

Ken went red. "I know. It came out sounding like something I never meant. I guess that's why Myra's always jumping on me. I have a way of putting things wrong." He glanced at her. "I would give a lot to get through one day without a blast from Myra. Think I can make it?"

Patty suddenly felt warm and friendly toward Ken. "I'm in a position to tell you that you've got every chance," she assured him. Now if that didn't stir things up a little between Ken and Myra, they were beyond help!

It was not like Guy not to be in touch. Patty still needed him for the Cokes, but he didn't stop in until the following Thursday. He said he was sorry but he would have to let them down. The friends who had helped him collect in the past were all busy.

"But we could help you—" Patty began.

Guy looked upset. "It's not just that. We ran into a little trouble from the store owners. They did not seem interested any more in helping Lane's End. They said it wasn't—well, what's the difference."

Myra folded her arms and looked at him. "Come on, Guy, they said it wasn't what?"

"They said it wasn't doing anything for the neighborhood people, so why should they do anything for it?"

Patty didn't say much as Myra told the boys that they would have to scratch for their own food this time. She was annoyed with herself for feeling that Guy had let her down. Not Lane's End—her, personally, as if he was no longer interested in her.

In the end they all went out collecting, and they were surprised by what they got. They came back with the car fairly well filled, and most of the store owners had seemed perfectly willing to contribute. Maybe, Patty thought, Guy had gone to different stores. Nobody really knew.

As before, the basketball game drew a lively audience, and after the young ones went home there were quite a number of young people left for the dancing. Patty got the impression that nobody was worried any more about a Lane's End party being watched by the police.

"As if everybody knows now who took the money, so the heat is off," Ken said.

"Nobody actually knows who swiped the money," Myra snapped.

"Nobody can prove it. But really, Myra, Terry—" Ken was stopped by Myra's icy glare, but he merely grinned, held out his hand to Myra, and said, "Want to dance?" They moved into the crowd.

"Well, what do you know," John said. "Maybe the last few weeks haven't been a total waste at that."

More than ever the Vistas and John felt their fight-back program was the right one. Patty decided that she would pin Amalia down to a definite set-up for her plant medicine talks. Even Grace agreed that maybe Lane's End wasn't on its last legs after all. She was helping the Vistas take down the paper flowers when suddenly she froze, her eyes glued to a corner of Eddy's painting. She turned a dark red and stalked out.

"What on earth . . . ?" John went over to see what it was all about. It was Eddy's picture, just as it had always been. Then Patty exclaimed, "Good grief!" and put her finger on a tiny spot—a small face so woven into the colors around it that it was hard to make out.

But once you saw it there was no doubt what it was—an ugly drawing of Grace's head. And underneath it, in small letters that Patty was sure had not been there before, someone had printed: *Grace Pascoe is a fatheaded fink.*

"Who would do that?" Patty gasped.

"Who did the rest of it?" Myra came back. "No wonder she looked as if she had been kicked in the teeth. If I get my hands on that Eddy, I—" She made a twisting motion.

CHAPTER 11

THE WASTE BASKET

"Grace is pretty sensible. She won't make a big thing out of this," Ken said, but he was nervous.

"You didn't see her face," Patty said. "It's Eddy, remember—the one she's really been pulling for. She thought they were friends."

John agreed. "Eddy's little fun might turn out to be Grace's big trouble. I know she would be happy if she could put even a single kid on the right track. If she fails with Eddy too. . . ."

Patty sighed, got up, and emptied the plate they were using for an ash tray. They had all been too nervous about Grace to call it a night. With surprise she found even she was holding a cigarette, though she seldom smoked.

"John," Myra said after a silence, "do you think the bad luck and the missing money and everything else that's happened are all connected?"

John shook his head. "I honestly don't. A lot of bad breaks, yes—but accidents."

"I think they are connected," Myra announced. "Remember one of us once said somebody doesn't want us around."

"Next we will be calling in the FBI," Ken said. But Patty found herself agreeing with Myra. She remembered the words Terry had let slip: ". . . I wasn't supposed to be here."

"All right," John said. "Suppose we go along with Myra for a minute. Who's behind it?"

"Amalia," Patty said. She had said the name without thinking. Everyone looked at her. She went on slowly, "It's just a feeling. She would have reasons. Being afraid her customers would turn to regular doctors. And that back room of hers . . . Lane's End could have become— I mean could become—her competition."

"But, as they say in the Westerns, you speak with forked tongue," Ken objected. "If she's our enemy, why do we want her on our team?" Then he looked up. "Patty, you've been brilliant! Of course! If you can't lick them, join them!"

Patty went to see Amalia the next afternoon, armed with a pad and a list of possible dates for Amalia's talks. She was making a friend out of someone who at the very least didn't like Lane's End.

It was an important visit, for Amalia chased out a few boys from her back room and invited Patty in. Amalia's living arrangements were clean, spare, and very simple. Draped over a chair in one corner, however, was a splash of brilliant material. "For the *fiesta*," Amalia explained when Patty admired it. "I will make new window curtains for the shop."

Patty did not know about the local *fiesta*, an end-of-summer street fair which was always held right in the alley. "It is the big local party," Amalia said. "Everyone looks forward to it, everyone comes. I am surprised you have not heard about it."

Patty and Amalia spent an hour setting up a list of talks about herbs. Then Amalia made some herb tea as a sample. One of her talks would be about the great variety of delicious and healthy "tea" drinks that could be made from different kinds of leaves.

Some noises came from down below, scraping and thumping noises that Patty remembered hearing before. "My neighbors. They rent my basement for storing extra supplies," Amalia explained. With a faint smile, she nodded toward her sewing machine. "Also, I sew a little for those who have no machines. It all brings in a bit of extra money."

Patty had never thought to ask Grace about paying Amalia for her talks! Were they going to bog down in red tape about who should pay for what, and how much, and spoil her beautiful idea?

There was a strange car in the drive when she got back to Lane's End. She was just inside when Ken came out of the office and pulled her quickly into the library.

"Shush!" he ordered as she started to speak. "Tell me something, fast. You don't smoke, do you?" Patty's mouth fell open. "Grass. Tea. Pot." Ken shook her. "Marijuana, you dumb bunny. Just say yes or no—I have to know!"

"No! And what in the—"

"Not so loud! Because somebody has said we did, that's what!"

She had no chance to pull herself together before he was rushing her into Grace's office, where she met Mr. Grant, a Vista director from New York. Mr. Nelson, from the church board, was also there.

"Will you all calm down and listen?" Mr. Grant said quietly. "You are not being accused of anything. But there's something going on that must be checked out. You will admit that Vista can't simply drop the problem."

"You have no problem!" Grace said. "I would stand up for these young people."

Mr. Grant shook his head. "I would stand up for them too. By the time our workers are trained we have a good idea what kind of people they are. But we three" —he included Mr. Nelson in his glance—"have lived long enough to know that impossible things happen every day."

"They've all denied it," John said. "We believe them. What more can they do?"

Mr. Nelson looked at the three Vista workers. "You are going to have to provide proof, I'm afraid," he said. "You are going to have to allow Mr. Grant to make sure for himself that no one at Lane's End has any of this stuff."

Myra jumped up, her cheeks flaming. "You want to search our rooms, isn't that it? What are you waiting for?" She turned to the others. "Does either of you refuse to let his room be searched?"

"Refuse! I will make them go over every inch of it." Ken said. "Let's get it over right now!" Then he stopped and turned to Mr. Grant. "How did you find out about this, anyway? Why did you come here?"

Mr. Grant explained that someone, in some manner he would not go into, had informed the New York Vista office that every kid in the neighborhood of Lane's End House knew that if they wanted marijuana they could get it there, from one of the Vistas.

"Why stop at marijuana?" Ken said. "That's small potatoes! What happened to LSD? Why not come in here and say we are shooting speed? Come in—let's get this search over with!"

Neither Mr. Grant nor Mr. Nelson knew exactly how to search a room. They kept saying, "Do you mind if we open that drawer?" or "Need we look on that shelf?"

Myra, whose room was first, marched around it with set lips, flinging open closet doors, dumping dresser drawers of underwear and sweaters on the bed, insisting that they move the bed aside to make sure nothing was hidden under it.

Patty followed her lead. She even handed her waste-basket to John so he could save Mr. Grant the dirty job of pawing through it. She was starting to pull open her dresser drawers when the sight of John's face in the mirror stopped her. He raised his head and met her eyes.

John just stood there, holding the wastebasket as if it burned his hands—and not only Patty but everyone else knew he had found something. Then he reached inside and picked out the remains of one of last night's ciga-rettes.

Even to Patty, who almost never smoked, it looked different. It was loose, flat, a strange shape. The paper was odd. John said, "I'm afraid this is what you are looking for."

Patty and Myra had never, to their knowledge, seen a "joint." But one by one the others handled and smelled it and agreed that it was indeed marijuana. Patty felt as if she had been punched in the stomach. She stood by while they went through her dresser and found three more cigarettes tucked between her things.

In grim silence, they went down to Ken's room and

found a small packet of the stuff rolled up in a sweater on his closet shelf.

Grace was the first to speak. "It's a bad dream," she said.

"I'm afraid not." Mr. Nelson's voice was cold and final. "These—objects—are real enough. We will need a few more words with your young people."

"Have all you want, and they'll add up to the same answer. These are not ours," Ken said. "We did not put them here. We were smoking in Patty's room last night, but not one of us had, or held, or smoked one of these. It's crazy, Mr. Nelson! It couldn't have been done without the rest of us knowing. Maybe the girls wouldn't have recognized it, but I'm no babe in the woods and neither is John."

"Except that if it was you or me, we would hardly have called attention to it," John said. He spoke in a bitter voice, and behind his glasses his blue eyes looked unhappy. "Mr. Nelson, Mr. Grant—we can't explain this now. But on our word of honor, we know nothing about this stuff. I can't imagine how it got here."

"Can't you?" Myra suddenly spoke up. "I can! What more proof do you need that *someone* is behind all the things that have happened?"

Of that whole strange afternoon, perhaps the strangest moment came when Mr. Grant and Mr. Nelson were leaving. It was clear that if it had been up to Mr. Nelson, they would all have been out on their ears, Lane's End closed, and maybe even reported to the police. It was Mr. Grant who saved them.

"It's a crazy thought—that Lane's End might have a local enemy," he told them. "But it's a crazy world. Things that can't happen have a way of suddenly doing just that. I've seen marijuana here, yes, but I'm not convinced one of you is responsible. Until I am, you've got some time to get to the bottom of it."

"You mean you're taking no action?" A little color came back into Grace's gray-white face.

Mr. Grant nodded. "But *you* must, Mrs. Pascoe. If this stuff was planted here, it's in your lap—all of you— to find out who and why. Otherwise . . ."

Otherwise they would be in trouble about as deep as they could be.

"One thing we won't do," John said later, "is cut back on our programs. If anything, we will double our efforts. The more people we can get to come in, the more we ourselves get around, the better chance we will have to spot whoever is after us."

But Ken raised a point that had been bothering Patty too: the more people who came around, the more chance there was for things to happen. "We are so wide open," Ken reminded them. "Except for Grace's office, and look what happened there. Anybody could get keys made."

They all agreed that they would be more careful, but that it was more important to encourage the feeling that Lane's End was truly a neighborhood place, open to all. Only not *wide* open.

They found themselves more eager than ever to get on with their projects, and decided to move them up. The fashion show would go on before school started. Ken and John would step up their "drop-out net," by which they hoped to spot boys who were hesitating about going back to school and herd them in the right direction. There were so many big plans—if only they could lick their problems!

They made their plans, but for several days they could get nothing started. The fiesta that Amalia had mentioned had the full attention of everybody, old and young, within range of Amalia's Alley or Lane's End House. Myra helped to make costumes for the children who would be dancing. Patty kept sampling food one of her girls' mother was making to sell at the fair. Ken and John worked along with the shop owners who were setting up their little outdoor stalls. Two musical groups were going to take turns for the block dancing. Even at Lane's End House the growing excitement was making everyone feel less nervous.

On Friday night, Patty dressed with more care than she had since leaving school. She wore a short, deep pink dress, brand-new, tied a matching silk scarf around her head, and found some eye shadow that was almost dried up from lack of use.

Myra had gone to a lot more trouble. She had set her hair so that it was a pale frame around her small face, put on false eyelashes, and was determined to leave off her glasses. "This whole summer I haven't felt like a girl," she said, "and if it's all going to end in some terrible disaster, at least let's have some fun!"

"I didn't know you ever thought much about feeling like a girl," Patty said. "You are so serious about social work—I didn't know you thought about much else."

Myra studied her lashes in the mirror to make sure they were still on. "To be honest, Patty, I never did before. But I have now decided to face a fact. I met Ken, I hated him—and I think about him all the time. Might as well get him out of my system so I can go back to putting my mind on my work, don't you think?"

CHAPTER 12

TRACKER IN THE FOG

The boys were using the station wagon for last-minute errands, so the girls set out alone. Grace had announced she was going to visit friends instead of showing up at the fiesta.

"Nobody will ever notice I'm not there if the rest of you are," she had said. "And I just don't have the heart for it. I've got to get away for a few hours."

But the Vistas were going to enjoy themselves. It was in the air all along Main Street. As they approached the alley they found themselves becoming part of a gay, noisy stream, all flowing in the same direction. Then, through the damp and fog, they saw the lights.

Fiesta! Across the alley, from one roof top to another, the shop owners had set up arches of many-colored lights. The stores, too, were brightly lighted, wide open, and the stalls outside packed with attractive goods. At the far end of the alley, the little rock group that had played at the first open house beat out a tune that had the younger crowd already dancing. Myra and Patty were separated almost at once by the shouting crowd, and the next time Patty caught a glimpse of Myra she was with Ken.

Patty was trying to head for Amalia's doorway when suddenly she was caught and whirled out among the dancers. Her body and feet had picked up the beat before she had time to look at her partner. It was Guy. Laughing, she felt herself caught, flung away, caught again, dancing as she was sure she had never danced before.

Then the second band took over and broke into a South American beat. Around them the movements of the dancing couples changed, following patterns Patty didn't know. "I can't do this stuff!" she shouted into Guy's ear.

"You don't think so?" He took a tighter grip and Patty found herself following him. Somewhere on the edge of the crowd she saw John looking rather worried, but she was too busy enjoying herself to wonder why. When the folk-rock group came back, though, she had to give up, out of breath.

"You are out of condition," Guy said. "You have not danced enough."

"I haven't danced at all since May," Patty admitted. "I hope I didn't get under your feet."

Guy laughed. "For a North American you picked up very fast. A little more time and I would have you dancing the Spanish dances as they should be danced."

Patty was faintly hurt. Why make such a remark when they had been having such a good time? She pulled away and started to walk off along the stalls.

Guy followed. "I am sorry. I was only teasing, but I see I do not really know how to talk to a girl like you."

"Oh, nonsense!" Patty said. "What do you mean, a girl like me? Have I got two heads or something?"

Guy said quietly, "Not two heads. But another language. We cannot understand each other."

"Guy, you are out of your mind!" Patty was confused. "You are talking perfectly good English to me. Better than lots of Americans I know. I understand you perfectly." For some reason she blushed.

He looked at her seriously. "You and I, yes, perhaps we could understand each other. But you could never know my world. Some of the things I have done you could never understand."

Patty was searching for an answer when John appeared behind Guy. "There you are," he said. "How about giving old four-feet a dancing lesson? You have a nice face and I know you won't laugh at me." The look he gave Guy had no laughter in it either.

Guy looked at him, then back at Patty. Once again,

as when she had first met him, he bent his head as though he were bowing and about to kiss her hand. "Yes. You will want to be with your friends. And I go back to mine."

"John," Patty said, "I could kill you. And I don't want to dance." He nodded, and they walked for a while until, on one of the food stalls, Patty saw cans of hearts of palm and other expensive-looking foods. "So I wasn't crazy after all," she said. "The Mendeses did have it."

John paid no attention to the remark. "Patty, it's none of my business. You are a big girl now. But Guy Delvarga—he's knocked around since he was maybe fifteen, and nobody knows much about how he's done it. He's different from anyone you've ever met before."

"Why do you suppose I'm a Vista?" Patty shot back. "Because I don't want ever to know about how people live, and what really goes on, and help?"

"Help Terry Mendes. Take kids to the hospital. Teach them to read. It's not your help Guy is after when he hangs around you."

"How do you know I'm not hanging around *him*?" Patty said in anger.

John stepped back. "Blow your stack all you like, but listen anyway. Guy lives by his own rules. And when it comes to girls, I don't think you'd like his rules." Turning sharply, he pushed away through the crowd.

121

Confused and unhappy, Patty turned and walked out of the alley, away from the noise and lights, coming out gratefully into the dark and quiet of Main Street.

Even the fog, heavier now, was nice. It made a sort of private place in which she could be alone. Why should John warn her against Guy? Guy had been a friend to Lane's End. Unless John didn't want friends for Lane's End. . . . Was that possible? Anything was possible, Mr. Grant had said. She tried to sort out her suspicions about John, but got nowhere.

Patty felt as if the fog were inside her as well as outside, hiding her thoughts as it hid traffic sounds and passing foot steps. She stopped to make sure of her direction. All at once her heart leaped. As she stopped, a sound behind her stopped too . . . another set of foot steps. She waited. There was absolute quiet. Then quickly she crossed the street, walked a little way, and paused again. Her palms tingled with fear. Foot steps— someone was tracking her through the fog!

As her own light steps picked up speed, the ones behind did the same. The short distance to Lane's End became a bad dream. Faster and faster she walked. The steps behind came faster.

She began to run. There was the street light that marked Lane's End. Heart pounding, legs going limp, she turned into the lane, ran blindly past the bushes,

gained the steps, was inside with the door safely slammed behind her. Then with a gasp she turned and double-locked the door. And listened. Outside there was absolute quiet.

Suddenly Patty saw in her mind something she had long forgotten—Guy Delvarga's slender figure walking quietly away from Lane's End in the middle of a dark night weeks before. Was it Guy out there? Had John been trying to tell her something she should have listened to?

Patty reached out and switched on the hall light. There was no sound except far away traffic. She took a deep breath, and counted to ten, and felt better.

All right—suppose someone had followed her home. Suppose it was Guy. He hadn't caught her. She was safely inside behind locked doors . . . the back door! She ran through the hall, through the kitchen, switching on lights as she went, and shot home the back door bolt.

Shivering, Patty made herself a cup of tea and took it upstairs with her, leaving lights on all the way. Shut into her own room, she felt more secure. The walls were protection. The door was heavy, the lock sound. Slipping through the bathroom, she locked Myra's door as well. Then she switched on her little radio. It was minutes before she realized some man was talking in Spanish.

Still in her clothes, she sat up against the brass head board with a book beside her that she couldn't read, still shivering in spite of the blanket she had wrapped around her. When the Spanish speech gave way to Spanish music, she reached to snap it off. She didn't need

Spanish music right now—to be reminded. Closing her eyes, she leaned back again . . . and then she heard it. A sound—not outside. Here in the house. Coming lightly, quietly . . . coming upstairs.

For a second she thought she might faint. Her mind refused to work. There was no escape from whoever was coming to her door. Then she remembered that all doors were locked. Better to stay where she was, not breathing, eyes glued to the door knob.

Another sound cut across the foot steps. Patty put a hand over her mouth and thought, "I'm making all this up! There's nothing down there. Nobody!"

But she wasn't a nervous girl, and she knew that what she was hearing was real. Only she couldn't quite make it out. A little thud—her ears began to ring with the strain. She put her head against the thick door. Silence. After what seemed like hours, she was certain that whoever had been in the house was no longer there.

She was almost too stiff to move when the others came home. But she was no longer on the edge of becoming a screaming wreck. Someone had walked behind her in the fog. Someone had been on the stairs. And then someone had stopped . . . or been made to stop. This much was real enough to tell them about.

As they had done once before, they went through Lane's End from top to bottom and found nothing.

They examined Grace's office, but the desk had not been touched. There was no sign that anyone had been after money.

"Call it a night," John said in a tired voice. "In the morning we can think about reporting it. Except that we haven't got a thing we can prove." He looked at Patty for the first time since coming home. "Unless there's something you can remember."

Patty met his glance. "I know exactly as much as you do. I heard someone. I don't know who it was, or what he—or she—was after. Do you?"

"Why on earth should John know?" Myra asked in surprise. In the same moment Ken exclaimed, "Say, what's going on here?"

Their puzzled faces made Patty laugh. She laughed and laughed—the strain had caught up with her. She heard herself say, "I've never fainted in my life, and it's not going to happen now."

"Glad to hear it," John said. He put his arm firmly around her and half carried her upstairs.

In the morning, however, they did have something to show the police. Under the bottom step where they had missed it the night before, Ken found a piece of thin black leather with black stitching. Nobody had to ask what it was. They had seen it too often on Ben Calder's hands. It was a piece torn off one of his gloves.

CHAPTER 13

THE WAITING GAME

"Nothing's turning out the way it ought to," Myra said later as they sat in Grace's office facing a police man. Officer Jim Meyer was questioning them, pulling out everything the police should have known weeks before.

Myra was right. A piece of Ben Calder's glove—and they should have had the answer to Patty's terrible night. It had to be Ben who had followed her home.

But it didn't work out that way. After they had called the police, John and Ken had gone out the back way to get the car and had stumbled over Ben's body, beaten and bloody and thrust behind the garage. He was in the hospital now, still unable to talk, badly injured.

Which still meant that the person in the house could have been Ben—or it could have been someone he had followed, fought with on the stairs, and scared away from the house before he could get to whatever he was after.

"So now you know this young lady was right," Officer Meyer said, nodding toward Myra. "Missing money, strange letters, planted marijuana—and you still couldn't make yourselves believe it was more than an accident?"

Accident! Patty had forgotten about little Joe, the night they had arrived. Officer Meyer added it to his report with a look that said, "Ah-*hah!*"

"You don't really believe the boy was pushed?" Grace asked. "Why, that would have been an attempt at murder!"

"We get them every day—murders," the police man said. He turned to Patty. "How fast would you say you were going that night?"

Patty looked at John. "Fifteen, maybe eighteen miles an hour?" John nodded.

"Well. So if the boy was pushed it was by somebody who didn't exactly want you to kill him. So what did they want?" He held up a finger for each point. "One, to scare him. Let's go along with what the boy told you, that it wasn't him they were after. So what have we got? It's *you* they want to scare. You, personally, or what you stand for, the settlement house. So I would say we have to find out who wants this place to get such a bad name that it has to shut down."

Officer Meyer watched them for a minute and then

announced that he would talk to them one by one, starting with Grace. Ken grinned as he got up to follow the others out. "That's so you can find out if any of us suspect any of the others, right?"

The police man grinned back. "I'm in charge, bud. I don't answer the questions. I ask them."

All the same, Patty knew it was true. She had had quite a few suspicions. Should she talk about them? No sooner had she sat down facing the officer's sharp but friendly blue eyes than she spilled every suspicion she had ever had about Lane's End. Including the odd feeling about Grace's way of doing things, about Amalia, about Ben, and even about John. And no sooner was it out than she felt better. It was nonsense to think John might have had anything to do with any of it!

When the police man left, they all lined up in the hall to see if they could guess if he was any further along. He returned and smiled at them all. "For the time being nobody around here is in trouble. You are a good gang. We've got to look elsewhere for the answer."

They made a stab at business as usual, but they were all relieved when only a couple of girls came to the library and a few young boys to fool around in the gymnasium. Several times they checked with the hospital, but by evening Ben had still not come to. In spite of that, they all, except Grace, decided to drive over to the hospital in case there was any further news.

Officer Meyer was already there. A lot of familiar people stopped by, asking for news of Ben—Terry and Vicky Mendes, several local store owners, some of Guy's friends, and Amalia. The Lane's End group had been there about fifteen minutes when Guy came in. Patty noticed that he did not come over to her—merely nodded, stopped at the desk, and then joined the three or four boys in blue jeans she had seen with him so often.

By this time there was almost a small crowd in the waiting room. John said suddenly, "Why are they hanging around? I've never known Amalia to leave her shop. And that drug store owner. And two of the boys with Guy Delvarga who should be at work right now!"

Officer Meyer's eyebrows went up. "Nail on the head, my friend. Why indeed? It would be more natural to just drop in, ask, and drop out again, wouldn't it?"

"They're waiting in case he comes to." Ken looked at Meyer to see if he'd guessed right. "That means they're worried about what he might say." Ken got what Myra called his "net-alert" look as he understood why the officer was waiting. "That means whoever did it could be right here with us!"

"If you don't keep your voice down you'll blow the whole thing," Officer Meyer warned. "Look, kids—a little

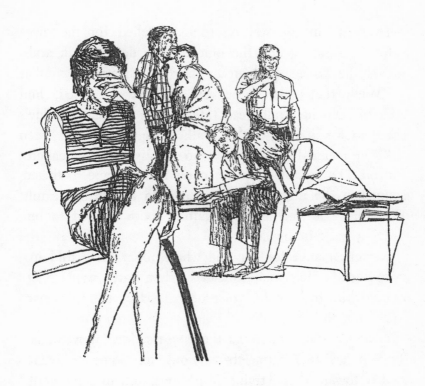

help! Hang around if you want, but don't cramp my act!"

Ten minutes passed. Patty went over to talk to Amalia. Officer Meyer's police partner came in, talked to Meyer, then left.

John had just suggested that they might as well leave, too, when the elevator doors opened. A doctor stuck his head out and motioned to the officer. Quickly, Meyer joined him. The elevator stopped at the third floor.

Everyone in the waiting room watched for the elevator to move. When the officer came down again and joined the Lane's End group they all stirred.

"Well, that's that," he said. As Myra gasped, he added, "Oh, he's not dead. He's going to make it. He came to for a minute, that's all. Long enough."

"You mean—he told you who it was?" Patty leaned forward. To be able to put a name and a shape to those sounds in the night, to put an end to that bad dream! Everyone who had left the waiting room seemed to be drifting back in now.

Meyer's glance took in the whole room. "He told us everything." He spoke so clearly that Patty wanted to remind him to keep *his* voice down. "He was awake just long enough."

Near the entrance doors there was sudden movement. Two police men came from nowhere. Someone went swiftly toward them, trying to get out, and in a moment the police men went down in a tangle of arms and struggling bodies.

"Wow!" Ken exclaimed, and he and John darted out into the thick of it.

Patty looked around wildly for Amalia, for Guy. Only strangers seemed to be pressed against the waiting room walls. Then the struggling group fell apart and quieted down.

First Patty saw Amalia standing by the glass door. Then she saw the boys in blue jeans being herded out by Ken and John and a police man. Then she saw Guy being held by the other officer. His dark hair was mussed up, his shirt torn. She thought, "He's always so careful about the way he looks! How he must hate standing there like that—trapped."

Myra clutched her. "Guy! I don't believe it!"

Patty didn't answer. She didn't want to believe it either. But she found that she had known almost from the moment the fight started that the person trying to escape would be Guy.

Officer Meyer wasn't answering any questions. "Lay off me now," he begged. "I will come around and give you the complete story later.

He kept his word. Around three in the morning he showed up, sure that there would be no sleeping at Lane's End that night. Patty had been as anxious as anyone, but when Meyer came in she suddenly wanted to get away. She didn't want to hear what Guy had done. She half got up, but Meyer looked at her. "You are almost more involved in this than anyone else. Don't you want to hear about it?"

"Me!" Patty sat down again.

"All of you," Meyer nodded, "but you especially. Remember we said someone was trying to put Lane's End out of commission? There could be only one reason—it was getting in someone's hair. Mrs. Pascoe started it when she began to make Lane's End over."

John still couldn't quite believe it. "You are saying it was a planned campaign to turn people against Lane's End?"

Meyer nodded. "But it didn't get serious until Mrs. Pascoe got herself a load of young people who actually started to get out into the neighborhood, out where the people lived. Made friends with them, got close to them."

"You are a girl who knows how to make people talk. That made her dangerous!" The words rang in Patty's memory. Guy had *told* her—and she hadn't understood!

"She was dangerous because Terry was so fond of her that she had been invited to meet the family, maybe to listen and hear too much. Guy couldn't allow that. The more friends Patty and the others made, the closer they might come to Guy's secret . . . Amalia's cellar and what was really stored in it.

"If it had been drugs," Meyer explained, "the police would have known about it long before. What was hidden in Amalia's cellar was food. Stolen food.

"Guy's racket had been beautifully simple. The food buying plan, which helped the poor families in the neighborhood eat cheaply, was also a money making plan for Guy. It started out quite within the law. He sold the food for slightly more than he paid and kept the difference. He was entitled to some profit—just as he was for his other activities, like finding stores to buy Mrs. Mendes' paper decorations.

"But Guy was out for bigger things. As he had told Patty, he had to find a quick way to make his mark and his money.

"If he could get food for nothing and sell it to his neighbors, he would make several times as much. So he and a group of his friends had started to hold up trucks. Working in the office of a big trucking company, Guy had a perfect spot for keeping track of large deliveries of food around the area. Sometimes Guy's boys went out alone. Sometimes Guy was with them.

"One thing that might make it go easier with them—they never used weapons," Meyer said. "We haven't got the details yet, but they would get the driver out of his truck somehow. They would fake an accident to make a driver stop. They would knock him out or blindfold him and tie him up before he got a look at them or their car. Then one of them would drive him around in circles while the others stole the food. They never took more than they could handle at one time, and the driver never knew what hit him, much less who.

"They had been doing this for a while before Mrs.

Pascoe came. But it was only when Lane's End began to make itself felt that they had to act.

"You three Vistas were supposed to start off with a real bang," Meyer said. "What an introduction to the neighborhood—to run over one of their kids! Yes, little Joe was pushed!" In a way, his quick words to Patty had started the ball rolling. Guy must have seen Joe and Patty together for a minute. Joe had been warned to keep his mouth shut.

"It got to be like a game," Meyer went on. "You made a move, he made one to check you. You give a big, successful party—the kids love it, maybe too much. So Guy arranges to lift some money. Every kid in the neighborhood knows the police will be extra sharp around here for a while, and they stay away. Don't bother about how he got into that bottom drawer. There must have been a hundred opportunities, and he had a hundred kids willing to do it if he didn't do it himself. He used them all as look-outs at Amalia's, you know—hanging around front and back.

"Most of the kids hadn't known what they were helping Guy pull off. But he had built up a kind of power with these people. He did things for their parents. They were proud to be on his team. It was a breeze for him until he got scared someone might talk.

"Terry had almost talked. She knew very little, but

136

there was no kid in the neighborhood who didn't know that there was something going on at Amalia's. Afraid that Terry's friendship with Patty would get out of hand, Guy had decided she must be taught a lesson. He had given her the money box and very easily forced her to hide—by threatening her with much worse if she didn't do as told."

"He must have been wild," Patty said. "Terry didn't obey him even as it was. She wasn't supposed to hide in my room. She must have been ordered to go somewhere else, and she didn't."

Meyer nodded. "Lane's End—and you particularly—threatened him. He got the marijuana hidden away to really turn the heat on. You all smoking in that room the night before just helped his plan along. And then you"—he turned again to Patty—"pulled a big one. You began to get cozy with Amalia."

"Did she know the stuff in her cellar was stolen?" Grace asked. "She's such an odd woman—but I can't see her doing a criminal thing, somehow."

"We will never prove it, but she's no fool. Guy paid her for the use of the cellar. But the odd hours they had to put the stuff in her cellar—she must have realized. Anyway, getting her to work with Lane's End was the last straw for Guy. He had to stop you. That's where Ben came in." He shook his head as they all sat up.

"No. Ben wasn't part of it. Ben doesn't want to be part of anything. He wants to stand outside and watch what's going on. But he found out that Guy was really going after Lane's End in a way that . . ." For the first time, Meyer did not seem sure of what to say. He looked at Patty. "Guy was going to make it look as if you were . . . as if you had . . . invited him here."

In the silence, Patty felt herself going red. But it was with rage. That was why Guy had hung around her! Setting her up! And she had been really interested in him!

Suddenly John slapped the table. "The hearts of palm! What dopes we are!" To Patty's gratitude, every eye turned to him. "That's how the Mendes family could treat Patty to that fancy stuff that Ken says costs a dollar a can! Guy couldn't always pick what he stole, right? So he sold it to the family for peanuts and it was still money in his pocket."

"Right." Meyer, too, seemed relieved to have the spot light turned off Patty. He explained that Patty had been followed by Guy. But Ben, already on to the fact that Guy was planning something involving Patty, had been right behind him. Evidently Guy had keys to every lock in the place. He hadn't stopped to lock the door after him and Ben had slipped in behind him. This was one time Ben had decided he couldn't stand by on the side lines—he had finally decided to pick a side.

Older and heavier, he had managed to force Guy out of the house. But then it was all over, because four of Guy's pals, hidden on the spot, had jumped him. "They thought it would be enough," Meyer said. "They figured if they threatened to beat him up again, it would be enough to scare him off. They were wrong. Ben would have turned them in no matter what."

Meyer glanced at his watch. "What a night! Might as well grab a bite and start right out again." But he seemed in no hurry to go and accepted with pleasure when Grace asked him to stay for breakfast.

There were still holes in the picture, of course, and some of them Meyer filled in as they ate. The day the station wagon had refused to start, when Tommy Pinello's life had been in danger—that had been Guy. Now that she knew, Patty saw it all. "Of course—when he sent me back up in the elevator and out the back way, he had time to run around the building and do whatever it was—"

"Pulled loose the sparks," John supplied. "I knew very well that hadn't happened by accident."

Even Eddy's attempt to hurt Grace with his picture— an attempt more successful than he would ever know— had been Guy's doing. Guy had convinced Eddy that

Grace had gone back on her promise to help him study art.

All this information hadn't come from Guy alone. The police had his four pals to question as well—four who were slightly younger. And once they had started talking they hadn't stopped. They would all draw pretty stiff sentences.

Pouring more coffee, John stopped. "Wait a minute. In the hospital, you said Ben was only awake for a minute. You never got his whole side of it in one minute!"

Meyer smiled, his eyes twinkling. "You are so right. At that point, Ben hadn't been awake at all. Guy fell for the oldest trick in the trade. He gave himself away when I said, in his presence, that Ben had spilled everything. But meanwhile Ben's been awake for some time, and he's told us all we need."

CHAPTER 14

FRESH START

Patty's heart was heavy after the officer left. Grace went to bed, but the others sat around talking over everything until they realized Patty wasn't joining in. Myra said, "We are beginning to sound as if we enjoyed this. I mean—Guy had his good points. Maybe Patty doesn't exactly enjoy kicking him when he's down."

Patty pulled herself together. Her anger against Guy was gone. She was remembering how he had talked about Vicky and making money—how sure he had been that for a young man like him, poor and foreign born, there was no straight way to get ahead. So he had picked a crooked way.

"Don't worry about me," she said. "Guy does have his good points, but my heart's not broken. No—" She shook her head. "What's important is that Guy is really just like Grace. They both see a wall between 'them' and 'us.' Grace would kill herself to help people—but her way is to pull them up into her world. She's always giving and they're supposed to be thankful."

"I'm getting it," Ken said. "I guess I've been that way too. Them and us—two different worlds. And my world is better and I'm doing them a big favor by giving them a hand up into it."

"Yes, and people like Guy don't want favors. They want to be looked at as people, just like any other people. Guy was terribly worried about the way his English sounded. He built it up into a big thing." Patty blushed but added, "I liked the way he talks!"

"And so did I!" Myra exclaimed. "You mean he didn't realize that it made a girl think of—oh, come on," she broke off as Ken and John burst out laughing.

"That's what I mean. He thought every time he opened his mouth we thought, 'Too bad he's one of *them*,'" Patty said. "Then there's Vicky Mendes—the way Grace never thought a neighborhood girl could offer something to Lane's End."

"Amalia was a step in the right direction," Ken said thoughtfully. "There must be others we can take. Instead of Grace's experts, couldn't we find some local people to come in and teach the others—maybe even in Spanish sometimes?"

John had been very quiet. Now he looked up. "I'm with you. I think we can turn this into them and us

together, but it won't be easy. I've seen all along that
the old charity way of thinking is all wrong. But I'm
not sure whether Grace can really change."

Myra got up and drew the curtains. "I will go beg

Vicky on my knees to talk to my girls," she announced.
"She sells in a dress department, right? She knows what
people buy. Maybe I can get one of my group to make a
career in fashion design!"

Ken got up, too, stretched, and started to clear the
table. "Maybe we can change Dead End House back
into Lane's End House, though I rather liked that scary

old name," he said. "Look—what are we all hanging around for? We've only got about ten months to put this deal over!"

Patty and John sat still. After a while she said, "Yes, but can we do it? Bring Grace around to a different way of thinking and build up a whole new program for Dead End—I mean, Lane's End—and sell it to the neighborhood? They might all be on Guy's side, you know, and hate us worse than ever. . . ."

"And squeeze more money out of the church board, and a few other little things," John finished. Suddenly he leaned over and patted her hand—the first time, Patty thought, that he had ever made a gesture in her direction. "I'm surprised at you," he said. "Let me remind you that Vistas don't ask such questions. They see what has to be done, think of a better way to do it, and then just do it!"

A damp dish towel, flung across the room, covered their hands. "Exactly," Ken said. "Like seeing what has to be done right now is a few dishes. Would you two kindly quit goofing off and let's—as you say—just do it?"